LONGARM DIDN'T KNOW WHERE THE BULLET WENT.

He was reasonably sure it hadn't come anywhere near him. A couple of strides brought him to Dewey's side, and without ever stopping he bent and scooped up the deputy, flinging him over his shoulder. Longarm staggered a little under Dewey's weight, but he managed to keep running. Another gun went off behind them, from the sound of it, Myra's Colt. Dewey yelped.

Handling Dewey like a sack of grain, Longarm slung the deputy over the back of the horse. Abigail grabbed hold of his belt with one hand to steady him and used the other to haul on the reins of the horse. The animal wheeled around and leaped into a gallop.

DON'T MISS THESE
ALL-ACTION WESTERN SERIES
FROM THE BERKLEY PUBLISHING GROUP

THE GUNSMITH by J. R. Roberts
Clint Adams was a legend among lawmen, outlaws, and ladies. They called him . . . the Gunsmith.

LONGARM by Tabor Evans
The popular long-running series about U.S. Deputy Marshal Long—his life, his loves, his fight for justice.

SLOCUM by Jake Logan
Today's longest-running action Western. John Slocum rides a deadly trail of hot blood and cold steel.

BUSHWHACKERS by B. J. Lanagan
An action-packed series by the creators of Longarm! The rousing adventures of the most brutal gang of cutthroats ever assembled—Quantrill's Raiders.

TABOR EVANS

LONGARM

AND THE
CHAIN GANG WOMEN

JOVE BOOKS, NEW YORK

This is a work of fiction. Names, characters, places, and incidents are
either the product of the author's imagination or are used fictitiously,
and any resemblance to actual persons, living or dead, business
establishments, events or locales is entirely coincidental.

LONGARM AND THE CHAIN GANG WOMEN

A Jove Book / published by arrangement with
the author

PRINTING HISTORY
Jove edition / October 1999

The Penguin Putnam Inc. World Wide Web site address is
http://www.penguinputnam.com

ISBN: 0-515-12614-4

A JOVE BOOK®
Jove Books are published by The Berkley Publishing Group,
a division of Penguin Putnam Inc.,
375 Hudson Street, New York, New York 10014.
JOVE and the "J" design
are trademarks belonging to Penguin Putnam Inc.

PRINTED IN THE UNITED STATES OF AMERICA

10 9 8 7 6 5 4 3 2 1

Chapter 1

Longarm stirred, stretched, and reached out to run his hand along the smooth flank of the naked young woman who was snuggled next to him. When his fingers arrived at the smooth swell of her hip and slid around it to cup her left buttock, she purred and rolled toward him. Her hand moved down and closed around his erect manhood as she began licking at the broad, muscular, thickly-furred plane of his chest.

Mornings look a whole heap better when a fella wakes up like this, thought Longarm.

He had to think about it to recall the gal's name, but only for a couple of seconds. It was Becky, he remembered, and he had met her the night before, while she was waiting tables at a hash house called O'Toole's in Fort Stockton. There was nobody named O'Toole; the owner of the place was a Chinaman named Ho Yun, who figured rightly that the workers from the Pecos & Sante Fe Railroad would be more likely to patronize a cafe with an Irishman's name on the sign. But he fried up a steak just fine and piled the potatoes high on the plate, and that was all Longarm cared about after a long, fruitless trip from Denver. The waitress, a pretty blonde who was as pleasingly plump as Ho Yun was scrawny, had made eyes at Longarm right from the moment the tall federal lawman walked in, and seeing as how there was no ring on her finger, he had decided that he might as well get *something* out of this trip to Texas.

Becky was pulling at his pecker like it was a balky teat on a milk cow. She lifted her head to look up at him and asked, "Are you going to stick this big ol' thing in me again, Custis, or what?"

He filled his hands with her ample breasts, cupping and squeezing the large mounds of creamy flesh. Her nipples were dark brown, as big around as half-dollars, and the buds at their centers stuck out a good quarter of an inch. Longarm took the left one in his mouth and swirled his tongue around it, then pulled gently with his lips and teeth. Becky arched her back and started pumping harder on his shaft.

Longarm lifted his mouth from her breast and warned, "Best go easy on that."

"Oh, no, Custis Long. You ain't going to go shooting off on me before we even get started good."

As she slid down in the bed, Longarm said, "Dang it, Becky—" but before he could finish whatever he was going to say, her lips closed hotly around his pole. He threw his head back and heaved a long sigh as she started sucking.

Becky spoke French about as proficiently as any gal Longarm had run into recently. He lay there and enjoyed it as she lathered up his shaft good and proper with her tongue, then moved her head even lower to suckle each of the heavy sacs below it in turn. Her hands strayed here and there as she feasted on him, her fingertips poking and prodding and tickling.

Suddenly, with so little warning that there was nothing he could do about it, those goading fingers had his hips thrusting up off the bed. Becky lunged for his manhood with her mouth and closed her lips over the tip of it just as his seed began to explode from it. His juices poured out into her mouth in surge after surge that sent shudders quaking through him. She swallowed eagerly, drinking down what he gave her.

Finally, Longarm's climax subsided. He sank back against the bed, grateful for the soft mattress underneath him and the pillow on which his head rested. His chest was heaving as he

2

tried to draw in enough air to fill his hungry lungs. A fine sheen of sweat covered his long, rangy, powerful form.

With a last flick of her tongue, Becky finished what she was doing and rolled onto her back. She spread her thighs wide and said, "My turn."

Longarm wondered briefly if it would do any good to plead for mercy. Deciding that it wouldn't, he dragged in a couple more deep breaths, then got on his knees between her open thighs. He put a hand on each leg and spread her even more. The triangle of blond hair grew long and thick and lush, almost but not quite hiding the folds of dark pink flesh with the enticing slit in the middle of them. Droplets of moisture sparkled in the early morning sunlight that filled the hotel room. Becky pushed her mound up at him and made a little sound of need deep in her throat.

He began by running a fingertip all along the folds, letting it penetrate just inside her. She whimpered again. Longarm probed a little deeper, but only a little. She was wet to start with, but the flow of her juices grew even heavier as he fondled her.

"Damn it, stick *something* in me!" she gasped.

Longarm obliged by plunging two fingers into her. Becky caught her breath and arched against his hand. Her inner muscles clenched around his fingers like warm butter. Her hips started pumping hard as he reached up with his thumb and began toying with the sensitive little button at the top of her slit while at the same time sliding his fingers in and out of her.

It took only a minute of what he was doing before she grabbed one of the pillows and jerked it over her head, biting into it to stifle the scream that welled up her throat.

Longarm didn't give her a chance to do more than draw a breath before he lowered his head between her legs and went to work with his lips and tongue and teeth. Her thighs clamped against his ears with passion-crazed strength, and he hoped like blazes that he wouldn't need to hear anything for the next few minutes. Or see anything, either.

She caught hold of his head with her hands and pressed his

3

mouth tighter to her. Her hips pumped up and down, her thighs scissored back and forth, and Longarm started to wonder if anybody had ever gotten his neck broken doing something like this. Then, with a moan that shook her whole body, Becky slumped back on the bed as if every muscle in her body had turned to jelly.

Longarm didn't waste any time congratulating himself. He was hard again, aching, in fact, so he moved up over her and brought the head of his shaft to her soaked gates. One flick of his hips sent him sliding into her, taking her by surprise as he filled her.

"Oh, my God! Custis!" she exclaimed.

Longarm didn't have any energy for talking. He was too busy thrusting back and forth.

Yes, sir, there was nothing like some hot, sweaty sex to get the day off to a good start. Right about now, Longarm was glad Billy Vail had sent him to Fort Stockton, even if the trip *had* been wasted as far as the government was concerned. . . .

"You ready for a break, Custis?" Chief Marshal Billy Vail had asked several days earlier. His tone was mild and friendly as he went on, "I know you've been mighty busy lately with some pretty rough assignments."

Longarm frowned in suspicion as he leaned back in the red leather chair in front of Vail's desk. They were in the chief marshal's office in Denver's federal building, and a glance at the banjo clock on the wall told Longarm that he was only about fifteen minutes late reporting for work this morning. For him, that was early.

As he cocked his right ankle on his left knee, Longarm fished a cheroot out of his vest pocket. He stuck it in his mouth, found a lucifer in another pocket, and snapped it into life with an iron-hard thumbnail. When he had puffed a few times on the cheroot and gotten it going good, he said ominously, "You ain't fixing to try to send me on a vacation, are you, Billy?"

"No such thing," said Vail. He picked up one of the documents on his desk, which was littered as usual with paper-

4

work, the bane of every lawman who had once ridden a horse but now rode herd on a bureaucracy. "This is a real job. But it ought to be an easy one. All you have to do is go down to Texas and pick up a prisoner."

Longarm clamped his teeth down on the cheroot to suppress a groan. "Texas? You know how blasted *hot* it is down there this time of year, Billy?"

"I spent some time in the Rangers, remember?" Vail said dryly. "I recollect it gets a mite warm in the summer. But you won't be there long, just long enough to pick up a fella from the stockade at Fort Stockton."

"A military prisoner?" asked Longarm. "Why don't they just court-martial him there and get it over with?"

"Because he's not in the army. He's a civilian."

"Then why's he in the stockade?"

"Because it's the army he stole from," said Vail.

Longarm shook his head. "I'm getting a mite confused, Billy."

"It's all in the report." Vail tossed the document across the desk. Longarm picked it up and started to scan it. "Simply put, this fella Rowlett was a businessman down there in the town of Fort Stockton, and he had a contract to supply the post with flour and sugar and other foodstuffs. But he never sold them a pound of flour. He sold them fourteen ounces instead, and called it a pound."

"Hell, Billy, this is just petty thievery," complained Longarm as he tossed the report back on the desk. "They ought to just fine him and send him to the local hoosegow for thirty days."

"You didn't look at the numbers. Rowlett pulled that stunt on everything he sold to the army, and he did it for five years. The army figures he defrauded them of over thirty thousand dollars."

Longarm let out a low whistle. "Well, that is a mite more serious, I reckon."

"Rowlett could have been tried in Texas, I suppose, but the Department of the Army wants him brought up here to Denver and tried in federal court, then sent to Leavenworth. I figure

5

they're trying to make sure all the other folks who do business with them know not to try to cheat them.'' Vail shrugged. ''So when the Department of the Army asks the Justice Department for a hand, we try to oblige.''

Longarm blew a perfect smoke ring, admired it for a second, then said, ''So I get the job of fetching him.''

''Ought to be nothing to it. Rowlett's not a desperado, just a storekeeper who got too greedy for his own good. You shouldn't have any trouble with him.''

''I still ain't clear on why he's in the stockade and not the local jail.''

Vail shook his head. ''I don't have that information. Maybe he's got friends there in town, and the army doesn't want to let him out of their sight until another federal man has custody of him. That doesn't really matter, Custis.''

Longarm uncrossed his legs and stood up. ''Reckon not.''

Vail nodded at the door that led to the outer office. ''Henry's got your travel vouchers. You can get to Fort Stockton by rail now, even though you have to go sort of roundabout to get there, so it ought to be an easy trip. No stagecoaches, no saddle horses.''

''Just a couple of days of breathing smoke and cinders and busting my rump on a hard wooden bench.''

''I declare, Custis, you're in a pessimistic mood today.'' Vail waved a hand at him. ''Go on and get out of here before I come down with it, too.''

Longarm picked up his vouchers from Henry, the pasty-faced clerk who played the typewriter in Vail's outer office, and didn't even bother to hooraw the young fella.

Texas in the summer, thought Longarm as he left the federal building and headed for his rented room on the far side of Cherry Creek. His boss sure had some damned strange ideas about what made for a nice, easy assignment.

Longarm had his weight distributed evenly on his knees and hands as he thrust into Becky. That was one of the keys to doing this properly, he thought. Good balance was essential.

6

"Deeper, deeper, you big son of a bitch!" panted Becky. "Give it to me!"

She said some other things, too, and the raw words that spilled out of the mouth in the middle of that pretty, wholesome face made Longarm pump even harder. He couldn't answer her plea for deeper penetration, however; he was already giving her everything he had. Bottoming out, in fact. Her legs wrapped around his hips and her heels thumped against his rump. Longarm wondered what was going to give out first as he kept pounding at her, the slats of the bed or his ticker, which was slugging a mile a minute in his chest.

A sudden cracking sound gave him his answer.

Becky was too far gone to hear it, and Longarm was too far gone to care. He thrust again and again and then started spasming, adding his seed to the flood that was already coming from her. She threw her arms around his neck and dragged his head down to hers. Her mouth plastered hotly to his. Her tongue speared into his mouth. He kept pumping through his climax, each thrust timed precisely with the jets of scalding juice. Becky thrashed and moaned as he emptied himself in her, but the contact between them was never broken. After the last shuddering spurt, Longarm finally collapsed, lying half on top of her so that his weight wouldn't crush her.

The bed hadn't fallen down after all, Longarm realized after a moment. He was mighty thankful for that. He would have hated to have to put the damages on an expense account for Billy Vail.

It was a few minutes before either of them could talk. Becky regained her voice first. Raggedly, between gulps of air, she said, "Custis, that was . . . just about the best romping . . . I've ever had in my life."

Longarm managed to prop himself up on an elbow so that he could look down at her. "Well, you're mighty sweet," he said. A grin spread across his mouth under the curling longhorn mustaches. "And I couldn't have done it without you."

She giggled. "Well, you could have," she said, "but it wouldn't have been near as much fun."

Longarm couldn't argue with that. He nuzzled her ear,

7

friendly-like, and she reached over to give his shaft an affectionate pat. "I'm sure glad you came to Fort Stockton," she said.

Longarm wasn't sure he would go quite that far—this role in the hay had been mighty nice, but other than that the trip had been a complete waste—but he was about to tell a white lie and agree with her anyway. Before he could say anything, however, Becky went on, "You're a whole heap better at this than Sergeant Mike."

Longarm frowned. "Who the hell's Sergeant Mike?"

He got his answer a second later when the door of the hotel room suddenly exploded open and a redheaded mountain fell on him, roaring all the while, "I'll kill the both of yez!"

Chapter 2

Fort Stockton had been established a couple of years before the Civil War, one of several forts built to form a line of defense for farmers and ranchers as Texas's frontier surged steadily westward. There was a good reason the nearby waterhole was known as Comanche Springs: That war-like tribe, the most feared in the whole Southwest, frequented the area.

The war had disrupted the army's efforts, naturally, but afterward, the blue-coated soldiers had returned to the Texas prairie, and with them had come more and more settlers. The town that had grown up around the military post had taken the same name, Fort Stockton. By now it was a bustling community. The threat of the Indians was just about gone, the railroad had arrived, and civilization was busting out all over.

The fort was laid out along the same lines as most other frontier forts. Frame and adobe buildings formed a rough rectangle around a large, open parade ground in the center. Longarm had seen hundreds just like it, and nothing about the place had struck him as unusual when he'd arrived there the previous afternoon. Challenged by a sentry, he had taken out his badge and identification papers and showed them to the young private, who looked like he shaved maybe once a week. The guard had turned Longarm over to a lieutenant, who promptly ushered him into the office of the post commander, Colonel Stilwell. The colonel, who reminded Longarm of a younger, scrawnier version of U. S. Grant, listened to Longarm's explanation of why he was there and then shook his head.

"I'd love to turn Rowlett over to you, Marshal, but I can't," said Stilwell.

Longarm frowned. "Why not?"

"The thieving son of a bitch is dead."

Longarm's eyebrows lifted in surprise. He repeated, "Dead?"

Stilwell nodded solemnly. "That's right. He was killed two days ago in an escape attempt." The colonel lit a cigar and added around it, "I can show you the grave."

"You may have to, just so my boss will be satisfied. How did Rowlett come to try to escape?"

"Desperation," sighed Stilwell. "He knew he was caught dead to rights and that he was going to prison. I suppose he couldn't stand that idea, so he jumped the soldier who brought him his dinner, overpowered the man, took his gun, and tried to make it to the stables so he could steal a horse."

"The guard went into the stockade carrying a gun?"

Stilwell grimaced. "I know, I know. And the careless fellow has been dealt with, I assure you, Marshal. At any rate, when some of my men tried to stop Rowlett and he started blazing away at them, they had no choice but to shoot back."

Longarm nodded and said, "Sounds reasonable to me. Reckon I'd have done the same thing in their place." It was his turn to sigh. "Looks like I came down here for nothing."

"I'm sorry, Marshal. No one expected so much trouble from Rowlett. He was just a greedy little shopkeeper, for God's sake, not some sort of desperado."

That was about what Billy Vail had said, thought Longarm. But almost every kind of critter in the world would turn and fight if it was backed into a corner, and that was what Rowlett had done.

"Rowlett's buried in the local boot hill," Stilwell went on. "I can have one of my officers take you over there...."

Longarm waved a hand. "No need. I'll find it. There's something else I'm curious about, though. Why were you holding Rowlett here at the fort? I would have thought he'd

10

be in the jail in town, since he was a civilian.''

Stilwell's lean face set in a tight, angry expression. "That was Sheriff Gray's doing. He wouldn't hold Rowlett unless the army was willing to pay a fee.''

Longarm had never heard of such a thing, and said as much.

"That's our good sheriff for you," said Stilwell. "He said that since Rowlett's offenses were committed against the army, the army would have to pay for his keep. Gray wasn't going to make Pecos County pay for it.''

"Well, I suppose a fella could look at it that way," said Longarm, "although it seems a mite odd.''

"If we had agreed, I suspect whatever fee we paid would have gone into Sheriff Gray's pocket, too." Stilwell clamped his teeth down on his cigar and added, "Forget I said that, Marshal.''

"Just because a fella packs a badge don't mean he's a hundred percent honest all the time." Longarm pushed himself to his feet. "Well, what's done is done. I'd better go take a look at that grave.''

"You're sure you don't want me to detail a man to go with you?''

"No need," said Longarm.

He left the colonel's office, and on the way out of the building he passed a sergeant who was going in. The non-com, whose thatch of flaming red hair stuck out from under his cap, was even taller and more broad-shouldered than the rangy federal lawman. And the glance he threw toward Longarm was none too friendly, either. Since Longarm had never seen the fella before in his life, he supposed the glare was just a reflection of the sergeant's personality. Anybody who had to wear those heavy woolen uniforms in this heat was liable to be a mite touchy.

Longarm had taken off the coat of his brown tweed suit, but he was still wearing his usual white shirt, vest, and string tie. As he walked back across the parade ground, he took off his snuff-brown Stetson and sleeved sweat from his forehead. The West Texas sky overhead was clear and brassy.

As he left the fort and walked the short distance back to

town, Longarm decided to pay a visit to Sheriff Gray instead of seeking out the cemetery, which could wait until morning. Rowlett wasn't going anywhere, and it was proper procedure, after all, to inform the local law of his presence in the vicinity. Besides, Colonel Stilwell's comments had gotten Longarm curious about the sheriff.

It didn't take long to locate the sheriff's office and jail. They were housed in a two-story building made of red sandstone, across the street from the county courthouse. Longarm went inside and found a deputy at a desk behind a waist-high wooden railing. "Help you?" the young man grunted without looking up from what he was doing, which happened to be studying the pages of an open copy of the *Police Gazette*.

"I'm looking for Sheriff Gray," said Longarm.

The deputy licked his thumb and used it to turn the page. "Ain't here."

"Where can I find him?"

"You can't, less'n you got business with him."

Longarm's patience had already run out. "I'm a deputy United States marshal," he snapped. "Now get your nose out of that paper, sonny, and tell me where to find the sheriff."

The deputy looked up in surprise and hurriedly pushed his chair away from the desk. "A federal marshal?" he gulped as he came to his feet.

Longarm flipped open the leather folder that contained his badge and identification papers. "There's my bona fides. Now, where's the sheriff?"

"I expect he's over at the Pecos House. He gen'rally takes his supper there in the dining room about this time."

"Much obliged," Longarm said. The deputy looked downright scared, he thought. He wondered if the fella had good reason to feel that way. "You nervous about something, old son?"

The deputy swallowed. "Me? Nervous? No, sir, Marshal, why would I be nervous?"

"You tell me," said Longarm.

"Everything's just fine, sir."

"Uh-huh," Longarm said heavily. He waited a moment,

looking intently at the deputy, then turned and walked out of the office.

Colonel Stilwell had implied that Sheriff Gray was a mite crooked, and the deputy's reaction to the news that a federal lawman was in town tended to confirm that impression.

But he wasn't there to clean up any local corruption. The citizens of Pecos County would have to deal with that themselves. All he was supposed to do was pick up a prisoner, but since that was impossible, he planned to head back to Denver first thing in the morning. He recalled from the schedule chalked on a board at the Pecos & Santa Fe depot that a northbound was due to come through at ten.

In the meantime, there was nothing wrong with indulging his curiosity.

He had already spotted the Pecos House while he was looking for the sheriff's office. The hotel was on the other side of the town square. Longarm's quick strides carried him over to it, and he was grateful for the shade as he stepped up onto the hotel porch. The sun was setting, but the air was still hot and would be for several hours yet.

There was a hint of coolness inside the hotel lobby, though. Longarm bypassed the desk and headed for the arched entrance to the dining room. He paused just inside the door and looked around, searching for somebody wearing a star.

A waiter in a brocade vest came up to him and asked, "Can I help you, sir?"

"I'm looking for Sheriff Gray," Longarm told him.

"Are you on official business?"

Longarm tried not to sigh. Folks around here sure tended to protect the sheriff from being bothered unnecessarily. "I'm a deputy U.S. marshal," he said.

"Oh. In that case . . ." The waiter pointed. "The sheriff is right over there."

Longarm saw that the man the waiter had indicated was already looking in their direction. As Longarm started across the room toward him, he came to his feet, and Longarm noticed that the sheriff's right hand was hovering mighty close to the ivory grips of the Colt holstered on his hip.

13

Longarm extended his own hand and gave the local badge a friendly nod. "Howdy, Sheriff," he said. "Deputy U.S. Marshal Custis Long."

The sheriff visibly relaxed and took Longarm's hand in a firm grip. "Ed Gray," he said. "Pleased to meet you, Marshal. What brings you to Fort Stockton?"

"A fella named Rowlett. Come to find out, though, he's dead."

Gray nodded. "Yep, that he is." The sheriff waved a hand at the empty chair on the other side of the table. "Sit down and join me, why don't you?"

"Maybe for a cup of coffee," said Longarm. He hadn't decided yet if he wanted to share a meal with Sheriff Gray or not.

The sheriff motioned for one of the waiters to bring a cup of coffee, then he and Longarm both sat down. Seated, they looked to be about the same size, but Longarm was an inch or so taller. Gray was older, in his mid-forties. His dark hair was thinning and had quite a few strands of gray in it. His face was rugged, like it had been hewn out of a cliff. Deep-set eyes, lantern jaw, strong chin. It was a face that could be brutal when it wanted to be, Longarm sensed.

The waiter brought the coffee, and Longarm said, "You don't happen to have a dollop of Maryland rye you could put in that, do you, old son?"

"No, sir, I'm afraid not."

"Well, then, that's fine."

The waiter went away, and Gray said, "Partial to Maryland rye, are you, Marshal?"

"Nothing smooths out a cup of coffee like a little Tom Moore," said Longarm. He took a sip. "But this'll do."

Gray pointed a fork at his plate, which had half a steak and a considerable amount of potatoes on it. "Sure you don't want something to eat?"

"Maybe later, after we've had a talk."

Gray grunted. "So talk. What can I tell you about Rowlett? The damn fool tried to escape from the stockade at the fort and got himself killed."

"That's what Colonel Stilwell said. He also said you wouldn't keep Rowlett in your jail unless the army paid you for it."

"Paid the county," corrected Gray. "And that's only fair, don't you think? Rowlett defrauded the army, not Pecos County. No reason why the county should be out one thin dime on his keep."

"Well, a fella could look at it that way, all right," Longarm said, just as he had to Colonel Stilwell.

"That's the way I look at it," said Gray, and he didn't bother trying to conceal the impatience that crept into his voice. "You federal boys sometimes forget how regular folks are just struggling to get by most of the time."

Longarm didn't waste his time or breath trying to explain to Gray that he didn't have much use for politicians or bureaucrats, either. He just said, "I ain't here to settle any disputes between you and the army, Sheriff. I was just sent to pick up Rowlett. Seeing as how he's dead, I thought I'd take a gander at his grave in the morning and then catch the northbound train. This is just a courtesy call to let you know I'm in town."

"I appreciate that, Marshal. You can see how I figured you might be on the army's side, though."

Longarm was tired of this. He didn't like Gray, didn't particularly want to spend any more time with him. He wasn't convinced the man was crooked, but his instincts told him it was a strong possibility.

"I'll be going now," Longarm said as he pushed back his chair. He dug in his pocket for a coin to pay for the coffee.

Gray held out a hand. "It's on me, Marshal. Least I can do for a fellow lawman."

Longarm dropped a dime on the table next to his cup. He saw Gray's face harden even more. As Longarm turned away, he felt the sheriff's eyes boring into his back. Could be he had made an enemy here tonight, but he didn't particularly care. After tomorrow he'd likely never see Sheriff Ed Gray again.

With his stomach starting to growl, Longarm went in search of a place to get some supper and found O'Toole's. He made

15

the acquaintance of Ho Yun and the pretty blonde waitress named Becky, and Becky suggested a hotel where he could spend the night. It wasn't quite as nice as the Pecos House, she told him, but Longarm assured her that was fine with him. She even insisted that he wait in the hash house until it closed, then she would show him where the hotel was.

Longarm was amenable to that idea, and so he had wound up with Becky in his bed, and she had kept him up half the night—in more ways than one. Eventually they had both fallen into an exhausted sleep, then woken up just as hungry for each other as they had been the night before. When they were finished, Longarm might have started to give some thought to getting up and finding that grave where Rowlett was buried.

But right about then, all hell had broken loose, and he found himself a mite busy.

Chapter 3

Longarm barely had time to shove Becky out of the way before the maddened sergeant came crashing down on top of him. She let out a cry of surprise and pain as she tumbled off the bed and fell hard on her bare rump.

The attacker's weight knocked the breath out of Longarm's lungs, and then his fingers locked around Longarm's throat. Longarm gasped and tried to drag some air past the throttling grip, but he failed. The sergeant's cap had come off when he came flying through the air toward the bed, and Longarm found himself peering up into a rawboned, hate-contorted face topped by a tangle of fiery red hair. The small part of Longarm's brain that was still concerned with such things recognized the sergeant from the previous day at the fort. Those same thought processes made the leap of logic that told Longarm this was probably the Sergeant Mike whom Becky had mentioned moments earlier.

At the moment, however, most of Longarm's brain was screaming for air, just like the rest of him.

He had twisted on the bed, instinctively protecting his privates, when he saw the sergeant leaping toward the bed. The sergeant had him pinned down, one knee on each side of Longarm's hips and both hands around his neck. As the whole room started spinning dizzily around him, Longarm reached

17

up desperately and grabbed hold of the sergeant's left ear. He twisted as hard as he could.

The sergeant howled in pain, and Longarm felt the fingers around his neck loosen slightly. He brought his other fist up in a short, hooking punch to the sergeant's belly. Longarm packed as much power into the blow as he could from his awkward position. The sergeant's grip slipped again.

Longarm writhed and shoved, and suddenly he was free. The sergeant toppled over the side of the bed. Longarm heard a yelp and realized he had just dumped the man on top of Becky.

Considering how the sergeant had looked so jealous when he came busting in, being on top of Becky was probably a position that was pretty familiar to him. But he had bellowed something about killing both of them, Longarm recalled, so he couldn't very well leave Becky to the mercy of the crazed sergeant. Longarm rolled the other way, which took him toward the holstered Colt hanging from the bedpost on the far side of the bed.

He got his hand on the smooth walnut grips of the gun and jerked it from the holster, but as he turned toward the other side of the bed, he saw that the sergeant was already on his feet again. The fella had one of those big, booted feet in the middle of the bed, in fact, as he lunged toward Longarm again. He swung a sweeping backhand that smashed into Longarm's wrist before the marshal could even bring the Colt to bear. The revolver went spinning out of Longarm's grasp.

The sergeant reached for Longarm's throat again, but this time Longarm was able to set his feet and meet the man with a straight, hard punch to the jaw. The blow rocked the sergeant back. Not much, but a little, and Longarm was grateful for any advantage, no matter how fleeting. He threw himself forward, tacking the non-com around the waist and knocking him backward so that both men fell across the bed.

More than half the slats broke with a series of sharp snapping sounds, and the bed collapsed, dropping Longarm and the sergeant into a heap in the middle of the wreckage. As he grappled with the sergeant, Longarm thought, not for the first time, how much he hated having to fight in the nude. It always seemed obscene somehow. There were plenty of things it was all right for a gent to do in the buff, but whaling the tar out of another fella wasn't one of them. Longarm threw a couple of quick punches that jerked the sergeant's head back and forth, then flailed his way out of the tangled mess of bedding and stumbled to his feet.

The sergeant was having even more trouble finding his footing. That gave Longarm a chance to club his hands together and swing both of them in a blow that had all the strength of his shoulders behind it. His fists crashed into the sergeant's jaw and stretched him full-length on the collapsed bed. The sergeant's eyes rolled up blankly, and Longarm knew he had a respite, of a few minutes anyway, before the sergeant regained his wits.

That gave him time to grab his long underwear bottoms, jerk them on, and snatch up his gun from where it had fallen on the floor. Then he hurried around the bed to where Becky lay huddled next to the wreckage and the unconscious noncom.

"Are you all right?" he asked anxiously as he knelt beside her. "Did that big yahoo hurt you when he fell on you?"

"I . . . I'm fine," Becky said through some sniffles. She looked at the senseless soldier and her eyes widened. "Oh, my poor baby!" she wailed. Heedless of her nudity, she threw herself on the sergeant and cradled his head in her hands, showering kisses on his battered face. "I'm sorry, I'm so sorry," she repeated over and over.

"What the hell?" muttered Longarm. Then understanding dawned on him. Becky and Sergeant Mike were lovers, but she didn't mind stepping out on him. Only when she did, he got furious and tried to beat to death whatever unlucky fella had been the object of Becky's dalliance, which in turn made Becky remorseful but also likely made her feel good that she could drive the sergeant into such a jealous frenzy. Longarm imagined that Becky normally tried to make it up to the sergeant by taking him to bed and turning him every which way but loose. The only one who really lost in the deal was the odd man out, who got a beating in exchange for romping with Becky. Longarm didn't figure many men would think it was worth it, considering the kind of pounding that a man like the sergeant could hand out.

"What in blue blazes is going on here?" a loud, angry voice demanded from the doorway.

Longarm looked in that direction and saw Sheriff Ed Gray standing there, gun drawn. Since Longarm was holding a gun himself, he moved slow and careful-like as he turned toward the sheriff. He held his hands well out to the sides so that Gray could see them.

"Reckon everything's under control, Sheriff," said Longarm. "But it was quite a ruckus while it lasted."

"I'll decide whether or not things are under control," Gray said coldly. He pointed his pistol at Longarm. "Drop that gun."

Longarm didn't let go of the Colt. In a voice as icy as Gray's had been, he said, "I don't cotton to having guns pointed at me by fellow lawmen, Sheriff. Maybe we better both just calm down."

"Calm down, hell," spat Gray. "I get reports that somebody's trying to tear down the second floor of this place, and I come in to find a busted door, a busted bed, a man who's out cold, a naked woman, and a man with a gun. If you can explain all that, Long, you go right ahead. But I'm keeping this hogleg on you until you do, U.S. marshal or no U.S. marshal." Gray snorted. "Hell, I don't even know for sure that you're who you say you are."

With an effort, Longarm reined in his temper. He didn't drop the Colt, but he picked up the holster and slid the gun into leather, still moving slowly and deliberately.

"You got any questions about who I am," he said, "you can wire Chief Marshal Billy Vail in Denver. Until then you'll just have to take my word for it if you don't believe my badge."

"Oh, I believe you, I reckon," said Gray. "But that still don't give you the right to disturb the peace in my town. I

20

don't know how Colonel Stilwell will feel about you assaulting one of his troopers, neither.''

Longarm drew a deep breath and said, "I didn't assault anybody. This fella is the one who jumped me.''

"And how does the naked woman fit into all this?'' Several people had gathered in the corridor behind the sheriff, guests and employees of the hotel more than likely, and they craned their necks to try to peer past him when he mentioned Becky and her state of nudity.

"He hurt Sergeant Mike, Sheriff!'' Becky exclaimed from the floor. "Arrest him!''

"Now, hold on just a minute—'' Longarm began.

"Maybe you better gather up the rest of your clothes and come with me, Long.''

Longarm stared at the sheriff. "You're arresting me?''

"I want to get to the bottom of this, and I reckon we can do it better at my office. From there, if need be, we'll go across the street to the courthouse and see the judge.''

Longarm's jaw tightened. He would have been willing to bet a month's salary that this wasn't the first such ruckus caused by Becky's overheated drawers and jealous beau. Gray had to have a pretty good idea what had happened.

But that wasn't going to stop the lawman from putting on some sort of dog-and-pony show that would wind up with Longarm being fined by the county judge for disturbing the peace. He imagined he would be assessed a hefty penalty for damages, too, and the amount would probably be twice as much as it would cost to replace the broken bed and repair the door. The extra money would find its way into the pockets of Gray and maybe the judge.

Back in Billy Vail's office, he had called Rowlett a petty thief for swindling the army. This racket of Gray's was even more of a penny-ante, pissant sort of deal, but Gray had already demonstrated he was the sort to grab every extra penny he could by trying to charge the army for holding Rowlett in jail. Gray hadn't made anything off that after all, so now he might be trying to make up for what he considered a loss.

"I don't think it's necessary to go back to the office,''

Longarm said. "I reckon we can settle this here."

Gray bared his teeth. "It wasn't a suggestion, Long. It was an order."

Well, now, thought Longarm, this was sure as hell a pretty little dilemma. And right now he didn't know how he was going to get out of it without either killing Sheriff Gray—or dying himself.

One week earlier

The wagon bumped and swayed, throwing its occupants back and forth with every rut in the trail. The two men on the box didn't seem to care that their passengers might be uncomfortable. In fact, the driver, a leathery old cuss with a bristly beard the color of ginger, seemed to be deliberately steering the wagon over the roughest stretches of road.

With each jolt, the younger man beside the driver smirked. He wore a .45 and was carrying a shotgun. The butt of the greener's stock rested on the floor of the box, and the twin barrels pointed almost straight up.

After a particularly rough bump, the guard leaned over and called back in a mocking voice, "You all right in there, ladies?"

Inside the enclosed wagon, which was like an oven with the sun beating down on it, Myra Dorn pushed a strand of fiery red hair out of her face and said bitterly, "I'd like to kill that son of a bitch."

"That's why we're here," said the dark-haired young woman who sat beside her, back braced against the sideboards of the swaying wagon. "I reckon we were both too quick on the trigger."

Myra snorted. "Hell, those cowboys were shooting at *us*!"

"Only because we were trying to steal their cattle," pointed out her partner in crime, Bridget Powell.

The other four women in the wagon paid no attention to Myra and Bridget. They were lost in their own thoughts, most likely brooding about how they had come to be here in this prison wagon with its single barred window in the door that opened out the back.

22

Sitting opposite Myra and Bridget, the would-be rustlers who had gunned down several cowboys in a running gun battle, were Abigail Ross and Deborah Fletcher. There was a strong resemblance between the two attractive blondes, so strong that it took only a glance to see that they were siblings. Deborah was single, despite the fetching beauty she shared with her sister, and Abigail was a widow, until recently having been married to a man named Howard Ross. She was a widow because she and Deborah had taken turns using a singletree to beat Howard to death, smashing his skull until it didn't even look human anymore. The way Abigail and Deborah saw it, it was only fair that Howard had been on the receiving end of the punishment for a change. There were still fading bruises on Abigail's face from the regular beatings he had handed her. She might have put up with that, but then Howard had caught Deborah, who lived with them in El Paso, alone in the house while Abigail was gone to the store.

Howard had long been of the opinion that since he was bedding one sister, he had the right to bed them both, and he had taken advantage of the opportunity to attack Deborah. The fact that he was drunk probably had something to do with the way he carelessly fell asleep after he was finished. He wasn't even able to fight back when Abigail arrived home, found Deborah devastated and sobbing, and went to fetch the singletree from the shed behind the house. The way the coroner figured it, Howard never really knew what hit him, and both sisters thought that was a damn shame. They hadn't put up any defense at their trial—in fact, they had admitted readily to what they had done—so now they were on their way to prison, having both been given life sentences.

Sitting with her back to the front of the wagon was a brunette who might have been young and fresh-faced and pretty only a few years earlier, before life as a soiled dove had put lines of hardness around her eyes and mouth. She was still pretty in a coarse way. Her name was Ginny Miller, and she made it a practice whenever she had a particularly well-heeled customer to slip a little something into the drink she poured for him in her crib. Then a male associate of hers would haul the soundly sleeping hombre off and dump him in an El Paso back alley . . . after, of course, Ginny had emptied his pockets.

It was a good scheme, and it had worked for quite a while, until Ginny had accidentally used a little too much of the knock-out potion on a visiting rancher. He had fallen into a sleep so deep that he forgot to wake up, permanently. And then his brothers, who were getting their own ashes hauled in neighboring cribs, had caught Ginny's partner trying to dispose of the body. In order to save his own skin, that fella had eagerly told the law about how the rancher had met his untimely demise, and in due course Ginny had been convicted of murder and sentenced to life in prison.

The only woman of the half-dozen in the wagon who *hadn't* been found guilty of murder, in fact, was sitting near the rear door, staring down at the planks of the wagon bed. Like the other prisoners, Timothea Jardine was wearing a shapeless gray dress, but something about her said that she was accustomed to much finer garb. Her light brown hair still had some curl and fluff to it, despite the time she had spent in jail and the two days she and the other women had been traveling in the hot, dusty prison wagon. Her skin was fair, her features delicate and attractive. It was that beauty, in fact, that was her primary asset in the confidence schemes she and her late husband had pulled off all across the Southwest. None of their marks had believed that a woman so lovely was just out to swindle them.

Their luck had run out in El Paso, where an erstwhile victim had figured out too soon what was going on and had had both of them arrested. During Arthur Jardine's first night in jail, a brawl had broken out among the prisoners, and Arthur had been in the wrong place at the wrong time. He had wound up with a makeshift knife shoved into his heart and died then and there, leaving Timothea a widow. She had been heartbroken, and the judge and jury had taken pity on her—but not enough pity to prevent her from being found guilty and sentenced to two years in the penitentiary. Timothea supposed she should have counted herself lucky: She would be out in a couple of years, while these other women would spend the rest of their

24

lives behind bars. But Arthur was dead, and that was all she could think of. Where in the world was she going to find another partner as slick as he was?

Each of the women wore an iron shackle on one ankle, and a thin chain ran from shackle to shackle, binding them all together. The chain was long enough that they could move around a little . . . if there had been anywhere to go.

The wagon lurched again, throwing the women back and forth, and Ginny said, "I'd like to take a hot poker to that driver's balls."

"I reckon if anybody would know what to do with a pair of balls, it'd be a whore like you," said Myra.

"Yeah, well, you and that girlfriend of yours sure as hell wouldn't," Ginny shot back.

Bridget caught hold of Myra's hand and said, "Never you mind what that trollop says."

Ginny straightened, sitting up from the wall. "Trollop, is it? You—"

"Why don't you just stop it?" Abigail said. "Why do you think they put us all in here together?"

"To save money," said Myra. "This way they only have to pay the driver and guard for one trip to the prison."

"But they won't mind if we fight all the way there," said Abigail. "In fact, the bastards would enjoy it."

"Mrs. Ross is right," put in Timothea. "We might as well try to get along."

Myra snorted. "Then tell the whore to be quiet."

Ginny's lips drew back in a snarl and she clenched a fist.

The wagon jolted again, and the back of Bridget's head thudded against the sideboards. "Ow!" she exclaimed.

Myra turned quickly toward her. "Honey, are you all right?"

Ginny shook her head in disgust and sat back.

Up on the box, the driver and the guard started singing a ribald song, making sure they bellowed out the verses loud enough for the prisoners to hear. They were only halfway through the song, however, when the driver suddenly hauled back on the reins and called, "Whoa!" to his team of mules.

25

He half-stood and peered down the road ahead of the wagon, then exclaimed, "Damn it! Looks like the bridge over Diablo Creek is out."

The guard frowned and asked, "Now what'll we do?"

The driver sat down and flapped the reins. "Best go take a look to be sure," he said as he reached for his whip to help him get the balky mules moving again.

As the wagon rolled ahead, Deborah asked her sister, "Why do you think we stopped?"

Abigail shook her head. "I don't know. It sounded like one of the men said something about a bridge."

Chains clanking, Myra stood up and went to the back of the wagon, bending over as she did so since the top of the vehicle wasn't high enough to allow her to stand straight. With her nose wrinkling slightly, Timothea moved aside to give her room. Myra peered out through the small, barred window, looking for landmarks. "I think we're getting close to Diablo Creek," she said. "There were heavy rains up in New Mexico Territory last week, I heard. The creek could have got up and washed out the bridge."

"What will they do if the bridge is gone?" asked Timothea.

"They can always go down to Springer's Ford," said Bridget. She and Myra knew this country the best of any of the women, since they had both grown up on ranches in the area before deciding that they had a hankering for each other and stolen cattle.

Myra turned around. As she took her place beside Bridget again, she said, "If the creek was up enough to wash out the bridge, the ford's liable not to be safe."

"Bridge could have been washed out for several days. The creek might have gone down enough to ford by now."

"Reckon we'll find out."

A few moments later, the driver stopped the wagon again and started to curse. Nothing was left of the bridge over Diablo Creek but a few pilings sticking up out of the swirling water.

"Looks like we'll have to turn around," said the guard.

"Turn around, hell! I'll go down to Springer's Ford."

The guard cast a dubious eye toward the fast-flowing stream. "That creek looks too high to ford."

"I been fordin' Diablo Creek since I was knee-high to a jackrabbit," the driver said with a shake of his head. "Don't you worry, I'll get us across."

The guard still looked doubtful, but he shrugged. The driver was older and in charge on this job. He'd go along with whatever the man decided.

Inside the wagon, the ride got even rougher as the driver left the road and turned south along the bank of the creek. "I was right," said Bridget. "He's heading for the ford."

A half-hour later, the guard called back to them, "Better pull your dresses up, ladies. They're liable to get wet." In a lower voice, he said to the driver, "Are you sure about this?"

The driver's weathered face was set in stubborn lines as he looked out at the crossing in front of the wagon. The creek was high and running fast, but the driver nodded anyway. "Damn right I'm sure," he growled as he flapped the reins, plied the whip, and then yelled at the mules until they strained at their harness and moved forward again.

With a splash, the prison wagon rolled out into the rain-swollen stream.

Chapter 4

"Shit!" yelled Ginny as muddy water came flooding in through cracks between the boards of the wagon bed. She hadn't heeded the guard's warning, and neither had any of the other women. Now they all scrambled to their feet and lifted the hems of their gray dresses, trying to keep them out of the water.

On the box, the driver worked the whip fast and hard, knowing that the most important thing was to keep the mules swimming. The force of the creek's current had taken him by surprise as it struck the side of the wagon, but he was still confident the vehicle could make the crossing.

"Hang on tight!" he called out to the guard.

The prisoners heard him, but unfortunately, inside the wagon there was nothing to hang on *to*. It was bare of furnishings except for the bucket in which they relieved themselves when they could no longer stand to wait for a stop. That tipped over almost immediately, spilling its contents and adding to the filthy flood, as the creek tilted the wagon far to one side. The water inside the wagon was several inches deep now, soaking through the shoes and socks of the prisoners.

"I'll kill that damned driver!" ranted Myra.

Bridget let out a moan of fear. "He should have waited for the creek to go down more!"

The two of them clutched each other, as did Abigail and

Deborah. Timothea and Ginny just looked at each other, neither of them wanting to reach out even in their fear. Then, suddenly, the wagon tilted even more, throwing all six of the women into a heap and tangling the chains that bound them together.

"Oh, Lordy!" wailed the driver as he struggled with the reins. The wagon was halfway across the creek now, but the current was even faster out here. With a violent lurch, the reins were torn out of his hands. "Jump!" he screamed to the guard. "She's goin' over!"

Both men went flying off the box as the wagon was flung onto its side by the torrent. They vanished under the surface of the creek.

Inside, water poured through the barred window and began filling the wagon even faster. The women shrieked and thrashed, clawing at each other and the sides of the wagon as they tried to keep their heads above water. The natural buoyancy of the old, dried wood kept the vehicle from sinking right away. Its weight dragged the mules right off their hooves, though, and swept the hapless animals downstream along with it.

The guard's head broke the surface of the creek. He shook his head violently to get the water out of his eyes and then turned just in time to see the wagon bearing down on him, less than five feet away. He shouted in terror and tried to dive so that the runaway wagon could pass over him, but he was too late. One corner of the squarish vehicle slammed into his head, crushing his skull and killing him instantly. His limp body bobbed along in the wake of the wagon after it passed him. The driver's body had still not come up.

The wagon twisted and turned as the current carried it along, so that the women were flung from side to side. Deborah was only half-conscious after crashing into the walls several times, and Abigail held her up as best she could. Myra and Bridget were hanging on to each other, and even Timothea and Ginny had forgotten the disdain that they held for each other. Timothea kept a hand gripped firmly on Ginny's arm. All six of them were soaked to the skin, their hair plastered to their heads.

The wagon had turned completely around now so that it was floating backwards down the creek. Myra was the closest to the door, and a glance through the barred window showed her that the creek had entered a canyon. Steep banks rose some fifty feet on both sides of the stream. The creek bed had narrowed down, too, which meant the water was flowing even faster now.

Suddenly, Myra's eyes widened. She saw a rock sticking out of the water up ahead, looking for all the world like a big, gray, jagged tooth. The wagon was being carried straight toward it.

"Hang on!" she cried in warning, for what little good it did.

The back end of the wagon crashed into the rock with bone-jarring force. For a moment, Myra thought it was going to hang up there, but then the wagon spun free and bounced away on the swift current. A couple of seconds later, however, with a less violent jolt, the wagon slowed again and then ground to a halt.

All the women had been knocked off their feet by the impact, and several of them had gone under the water, which by now filled more than half the wagon. Timothea came up sputtering and gasping for air, then realized she was no longer holding on to Ginny's arm. "Ginny!" she cried as she looked around and didn't see the prostitute.

Myra had hold of the bars in the window, jerking back and forth on them. "Help me!" she called to Bridget, who joined her. Several large cracks ran through the door below the window. Myra turned her head and said, "Come on!" to Abigail and to Deborah, who was starting to regain her senses.

The two sisters went to the back of the wagon and reached for the bars, throwing their strength into the effort along with Myra and Bridget. Meanwhile, Timothea gulped down a deep breath, then let herself sink under the water. The creek was so muddy from the recent runoff that Timothea couldn't see much of anything when she opened her eyes. She squinted and felt

31

around, exploring the part of the wagon where she had last seen Ginny.

Her hands brushed against fabric, and she clutched at it. She hauled up as she clambered to her feet. Ginny came with her, so limp that at first Timothea thought surely the soiled dove was dead. But then, as Ginny's head broke the surface, she gasped and sputtered and vomited creek water as she slumped against the side of the wagon. She leaned there for a long moment, then looked up at Timothea past the strands of sodden hair that hung in front of her eyes.

"Th-thanks," she said. "Where are we? Why have we stopped?"

"We're hung up on a sandbar!" snapped Myra from the rear of the wagon. "Give us a hand getting this door open before we float off of here!"

Ginny and Timothea stumbled over to join the others. They yanked and jerked, pushed and pulled, and with a cracking sound the door suddenly opened into the wagon, spilling all of the prisoners again.

"The lock got busted when the wagon ran into that rock!" said Myra as she scrambled up. "Come on!"

They all tried to get out at once, jamming up momentarily before spilling out through the shattered door and falling onto the sandbar. The bar was only about ten feet wide and thirty long, but it had been enough to stop the progress of the wagon.

The women sprawled on the sand for a few moments, almost overcome with exhaustion, fear, and relief at escaping from the wagon before they died in it. Myra rolled onto her back and breathed deeply, while Bridget lay face down beside her. Ginny coughed up more water. Abigail and Deborah sat with their arms around each other. Timothea was stretched out on her side, staring dully at the water racing by several feet away.

Someone had to take charge. Myra sat up and asked, "Is everybody all right?"

"I swallowed half that filthy creek," said Ginny. "What do you think?"

"I think you're damned lucky to be alive. We all are."

Myra pushed herself to her feet. "Come on. We'd better get in the center of the sandbar. I want to be well clear of that wagon if it floats free."

Grudgingly, the others got up. For a moment, they moved around each other gingerly, almost like they were following the steps of a dance, but their real object was to untangle the chain between their ankles. The chain began at Ginny and ended at Abigail, and the section between each woman was eight feet long. Once they were straightened out, they were able to walk fairly easily along the sandbar without tripping each other.

Bridget laughed hollowly. "Looks like none of us will be going anywhere without the others."

"Not until we get these chains off," said Myra.

"How are we going to do that?" asked Ginny. "Do you see a blacksmith shop out here?"

"We'll deal with that later," Myra said, her jaw tight. "First let's figure out how we're going to get off this sandbar."

She looked around and saw that a hundred yards farther on downstream, the canyon walls fell away. The creek widened considerably down there and grew more shallow, and the current looked slower. If they could reach that stretch of the stream, they could probably swim or even wade out.

She turned her head and stared back at the wagon. It was lying on its side, having dug a shallow furrow in the edge of the sandbar. It wouldn't take much to dislodge it, thought Myra. And suddenly she was hurrying back toward the vehicle, rather than away from it.

"Now what?" complained Ginny as she was dragged along behind Myra with the others.

The mules had all drowned, and their carcasses were already swelling. Myra yanked up her dress and reached between her legs. Ginny snorted and said, "You can play with yourself later, or have your little friend do it for you."

Myra ripped loose the short, slender dagger that had been tied to her inner thigh. She spun around and put the tip of the

33

blade to Ginny's throat. "Shut up, whore," she hissed. Ginny paled and took a step backward.

Myra had had the dagger smuggled into her jail cell in El Paso. She had paid dearly for it, and not even Bridget knew about it until now. But she had been unwilling to go to prison without some sort of weapon, and now, even though they were still hundreds of miles from the penitentiary, the little blade might still save all their lives.

The current was tugging at the bodies of the mules. Myra cut the harness so that they floated free. That left the wagon precariously perched on the edge of the sandbar. Myra jerked her head toward it and said to the others, "Climb on."

"What?" said Timothea. "You . . . you expect us to get back in that wagon?"

"Not in it. On top of it." Myra shot a glance at Ginny. "I reckon being on top's sort of unusual for you."

"But probably not for you," Ginny shot back. "What do you figure we'll do, ride this thing down there to where the creek's shallower and not so fast?"

"That's right. I'd rather do that than try to stay afloat in this fast current."

Ginny gave a clearly reluctant nod. "Might work," she admitted. "I'm willing to give it a try."

"So am I," said Abigail, and Deborah nodded. After a moment, so did Timothea and Bridget.

"Everybody climb on," Myra said again. "I'll push it free."

"It's liable to take two of us," Ginny argued. "You and me, Red, since we're on the end of the chain."

"Or us," said Deborah, "since we're on the other end."

Myra shook her head. "Get up there. Ginny and I will do it."

The two of them boosted the others, who climbed awkwardly atop the overturned wagon. "When we push it free," said Myra, "we'll have to jump for it. Be ready to grab our hands and haul us up."

The four women on top of the wagon nodded in understanding. Myra and Ginny spread out as much as they could and

34

braced their feet against the wet sand. They placed their hands flat on the top of the wagon and began to shove.

It moved only slightly at first, but the tug of the current helped them, and suddenly the wagon was floating free. "Jump!" cried Bridget. As the wagon began to pick up speed, Myra and Ginny leaped up, reaching for the outstretched hands of the others. If either of them failed to make it, they might drag all the others off and into the deadly current. The shackles and the chain would surely pull them down to their doom if that happened.

But hands grabbed wrists in firm grips, and Myra and Ginny were hauled up on top of the wagon with the rest of the prisoners. The six women held on to each other and the wagon as it shot downstream. The canyon closed in to its narrowest point just before it widened out, and the wagon had only a few feet of clearance on each side as it raced past the vertical sandstone banks.

Then suddenly the canyon ended, and the wagon popped out like a watermelon seed into the calmer water. There was still a current here, of course, but it carried the wagon and the women toward the shore. When Myra judged they were close enough, she called, "Everybody jump—*now*!"

They went sailing off the wagon and landed in water that came only to their thighs. Getting their feet under them, they stumbled up onto the shore, soaked, filthy, bedraggled—but alive.

And free.

Except for the chains.

Still exhausted from their ordeal, all of them slumped to the ground. It had been shady in the canyon, but out here, the sun was still shining brightly, and the heat soon began to dry their clothes. It also lulled them to sleep.

Myra woke up with a jerk after she had been dozing only a couple of minutes. "Get up," she said harshly to the others. "We've got to get moving."

"Why?" groaned Timothea. "I'm tired."

"We can't just sit here beside this creek."

Ginny said, "We can for a little while. What's it going to hurt?"

"I don't know, but I tell you, we can't stay here." Myra didn't know how to explain it, but her instincts told her that it wasn't safe here, that they would be better off finding some other place to hole up and rest.

"Myra's right," Bridget said loyally. "We ought to go."

"Well, I'm not going anywhere," said Ginny. "I'm staying right here. And as long as we're chained together, so will the rest of you."

"That's right, little missy," said a man's voice. "You ain't goin' anywhere. And if any of you bitches move, I'll blow your damn heads off!"

Chapter 5

None of the six women did as they were told. All of them turned sharply to look toward the source of the voice. They saw the driver of the prison wagon standing on a rocky knoll a few yards away. He was pointing his pistol, a nearly new Colt Peacemaker, at them.

"I said don't move," he shouted. The barrel of the gun wobbled a little. Like the women, the man's clothes were soaked, and he had lost his hat in the rain-swollen creek. A few strands of hair were plastered across his mostly bald head. He swayed a little as he stood atop the knoll.

"Put that gun up, old man," Myra called to him. "You're not taking us to prison anymore."

"The hell I ain't! I was paid to do a job, and by God I figure to do it! Ain't no bunch of ornery she-males gonna—"

His eyes rolled up in his head, the Colt slipped from his fingers, and he pitched forward face down on the rocky slope.

The suddenness of his collapse made Abigail, Deborah, and Timothea jerk back in surprise. Myra, Bridget, and Ginny stood their ground. When a couple of seconds had passed and the fallen driver still hadn't moved, Myra yanked lightly on the chain and said, "Come on." She started toward the driver.

The others had no choice but to follow. When she reached the driver, Myra bent over quickly and picked up the Colt. Getting soaked in muddy creek water probably hadn't been very good for the gun, but it would likely still work. Myra stepped back and trained the Colt on the driver. The man still didn't move.

"Is . . . is he dead?" asked Deborah.

"We'll find out," said Ginny. She went to her knees beside the driver and reached out to check his neck for a pulse. After a moment she looked up at the others and shook her head. "Dead as he can be."

Myra reached down and gingerly felt of the old man's skull. "Got a caved-in place back here," she said. "He probably hit it on a rock in the creek. Either that, or a mule's hoof or the wagon clipped him when he jumped off. He was walking around dead and just didn't know it yet."

Timothea hugged herself, and both Abigail and Deborah shuddered. They were all strangers to violence; the only other dead man the sisters had ever seen was Howard Ross, and they had killed him themselves.

Myra didn't seem particularly bothered by the driver's death. She broke open the Colt and removed the cylinder. "We'll need to let this dry out good," she said. "Bridget, get the shell belt off him."

"You're taking the gun?" asked Timothea.

Myra snorted. "Damn right. We're miles from anywhere, in some of the worst country in West Texas." She looked around at the surrounding terrain and pointed to a range of low peaks to the north. "That'd be the White Mountains over yonder. Not much in the way of water or anything else up that way. Over to the south, though, those are the Davis Mountains. There are ranches down there. If we can find one of them, we can maybe get rid of these chains, find some better clothes, and get our hands on some horses."

"Steal them, you mean," said Ginny.

"Don't get all high and mighty on me," snapped Myra. "It ain't like what you've been doing the past few years is the same as singing hymns in church."

Bridget tried to strap the shell belt she had taken off the driver around her own waist. She was a little thick through

38

the middle, though, and the belt wouldn't buckle. "It's too small," she said.

Myra held out a hand. "I'll try it." She took the belt and buckled it on. It fit fine. "Let's go."

Abigail gestured at the dead man. "Are we just going to leave him here?"

"You feel like scratching out a hole for him in this rocky ground with nothing but your fingernails?"

Abigail hesitated, but only for an instant before shaking her head.

"Well, neither do I," said Myra. "Come on."

Leaving the dead man behind, the six women began trudging south, following the eastern bank of Diablo Creek.

Fort Stockton

Longarm was still trying to figure out a way to keep Sheriff Gray from taking him to jail without bloodshed, when running footsteps suddenly sounded in the hallway outside the hotel room. "Sheriff! Sheriff!" called a familiar voice. "Got an important telegram for you from El Paso!"

Gray jerked a look over his shoulder and exclaimed, "Damn it, Dewey! I'm holding a gun on a man here! Don't come up behind me yelling like that!"

"But the wire's from the sheriff over in El Paso. He said to get the news to you right away," protested Dewey. "He said you'd want to know about it."

"Know about *what*?" Gray practically roared.

"The fugitives. There's half a dozen of 'em on the loose, somewhere over here in Pecos County."

Gray's gun lowered toward the floor, and Longarm relaxed—a little. "What the hell are you talking about?" demanded Gray.

Dewey came into view, and Longarm recognized him as the deputy he had seen in the sheriff's office the day before. The young man was slender, with an earnest face and a wispy mustache. He thrust a yellow flimsy from the telegraph office toward the sheriff.

"Six prisoners escaped from the prison wagon takin' them

to the penitentiary," Dewey explained. "Killed the driver and the guard and disappeared."

Gray lowered his gun even more and used his other hand to snatch the flimsy from Dewey. "Let me see that!"

As Gray scanned the words on the telegram, Longarm asked dryly, "Does this mean you and me ain't going to have ourselves a shoot-out after all, Sheriff?"

"Shut up, Long."

Longarm could have taken offense at that, but he decided not to. Instead he reached for his trousers and shirt. He pulled on the trousers and then buckled the shell belt with its crossdraw rig around his hips. As he shrugged into the shirt and began to button it, the sergeant gave a moan from the floor.

"Mike!" exclaimed Becky. "Speak to me, Mike!"

"He'll be all right," Longarm told her. He tucked the shirt into his trousers. "He was just knocked out."

Becky glared up at him. "You didn't have to hit him so hard!"

"Seemed like the thing to do at the time," said Longarm. "Besides, you didn't have to wind up in my bed, neither. I don't recall forcing you."

"You seduced me, you . . . you big city mountebank!"

It was a good word, thought Longarm, even if it didn't quite fit. He wasn't in any mood to give the gal a vocabulary lesson, however. He said, "This is the Sergeant Mike you were talking about, ain't it?"

"That's right." Becky sniffed.

"And he fancies himself your fella."

"He *is* my fella. He treats me nicer than anybody else around here."

"Then why do you go off with other gents?"

"Well, he's busy at the post a lot. . . ." Becky's glare deepened. "You're acting like this is all my fault!"

Longarm rolled his eyes and turned back toward Sheriff Gray. The local lawman had holstered his gun, Longarm saw. Gray was rereading the telegram.

"What about all this?" asked Longarm, waving a hand at the still recumbent Sergeant Mike and the broken bed.

40

Gray barely glanced at him. "Oh, that." The sheriff shook his head. "Never mind about that. I'll talk to Stilwell, and he'll take the damages out of Flaherty's pay like before."

"Then this ain't the first time such a ruckus has happened?"

"Good Lord, no." Gray jerked his chin toward Becky. "Any halfway good-looking stranger comes into town, she's got her drawers off inside an hour."

"Sheriff!" Becky exclaimed in outrage. "How can you say such a mean thing? And after all we've meant to one another—"

"Hush up about that," Gray said hurriedly.

Glad that fate had intervened and saved him from a possible corpse-and-cartridge session with another badge-toter—even a semi-crooked one—Longarm gestured toward the telegraph flimsy and asked, "What's that all about?"

Dewey began eagerly, "Escaped prisoners—"

"Go on back to the jail," Gray interrupted. "Can't leave the office unattended."

"But, Sheriff," argued Dewey, "don't we need to start getting a posse together?"

"I'll think on it. Now get on back to the jail like I told you!"

Dewey ducked his head, shame-faced from the scolding, and hurried away down the hall. Gray turned back to Longarm and said, "Why don't you come on over to the Pecos House with me? We'll get some breakfast and hash this out."

"Sounds good," Longarm agreed.

"I know you're a federal man and this is a state matter, but I wouldn't mind a word or two of advice."

The almost complete reversal of Gray's attitude might have taken Longarm by surprise, had he not seen the light of avarice begin to burn in the sheriff's eyes as he read the telegram from El Paso. Gray saw some sort of money-making angle in this incident, and that was why he was willing to forget about the destruction in the hotel room. Now he was after a bigger payoff than he could get by shaking down Longarm.

Longarm pointed a thumb at the still-naked Becky and the

41

groggy Sergeant Mike, who was now trying unsteadily to sit up. "What about those two?"

"I'll send a man out to the post to tell Colonel Stilwell what happened. He'll have some of his soldiers come and haul Flaherty off to the stockade."

Becky began to sob again. "It's not Mike's fault," she wailed. "He shouldn't have to go to the stockade."

"Take that up with the colonel," Gray told her coldly.

Longarm pulled on his socks and stomped his feet down in his boots, then stuffed his vest and string tie into his warbag. His Stetson had gotten knocked to the floor. He picked it up, adjusted the crown, and clapped it on.

Gray said, "All right, break it up," to the bystanders lingering in the hotel corridor. He led Longarm to the stairs. They went down, through the narrow lobby, and along the street to the much more opulent Pecos House.

The dining room was almost full, but Longarm noticed that the best table was sitting empty. It came as no surprise to him when the waiter ushered him and Sheriff Gray over to it. "I see they hold your place for you," he commented as they sat down.

Gray nodded. "They know I'm a good customer."

Longarm would have wagered that it had been a long time since Gray had actually paid for a meal anywhere in this town, but he kept that thought to himself. Now that Gray was being civil to him again, he didn't want to start another ruckus.

"Bring us a pot of coffee, a couple of steaks each, and all the fried eggs and hash browns you can get on the plate. And keep the coffee coming," Gray said to the waiter, who nodded and hurried toward the kitchen. To Longarm, Gray added, "Hope you've worked up an appetite." He grinned. "If you haven't, then Becky must be slipping."

"If I'd known that sergeant has his brand on her, I never would have dallied my loop," said Longarm.

"Done some cowboying, have you?"

Longarm nodded. "When I first came out here from West-by-God Virginia, after the Late Unpleasantness. And if you're

42

planning on asking me which side I fought on, don't waste your time. I plumb disremember.''

"I don't give a damn. War's been over for fifteen years, and I never made a dime off it anyway." Gray took the telegram from his shirt pocket and slapped it down on the table. "Read that."

Longarm read. The telegram was from the sheriff of El Paso County, as Dewey had said, and the deputy had been right about the rest of the message, too. Six prisoners, five of them convicted murderers, had been on their way to prison when something had happened to the two men transporting them in a wagon. The wreckage of the wagon had been found on the banks of Diablo Creek by a Mexican sheepherder, who had followed the creek upstream and found the bodies of the two men. From the damage done to the corpses by buzzards and coyotes, it appeared that they had been dead for several days. The sheepherder had told someone about his grisly discovery, and they had told somebody else, until the news finally filtered back to El Paso, which was the next county seat to the west of Fort Stockton despite the fact the settlements were over two hundred miles apart. Distance didn't mean a whole lot in West Texas, since there was so damned much of it.

Some of that Longarm read between the lines of the tersely-composed telegram. He knew how lawmen thought, having been one himself for quite a while. He pushed the flimsy back across the table to Gray and said, "I reckon this Diablo Creek must be in your bailiwick?"

Gray nodded. "That's right. I know where it crosses the old Butterfield stage trail, too, and that's the route those prison wagons usually take."

"So it's up to you to go after those fugitives."

"Yep. Want to come along?"

The offer was unexpected. Longarm said, "I'm a federal man. You said so yourself. Those prisoners escaped from the custody of the State of Texas."

"Yeah, but you're the first man to ever hold his own against Mike Flaherty. Hell, you did more than that. You knocked him out."

43

Longarm shrugged. "Lucky punch," he said, even though it really hadn't been.

The waiter arrived with a coffeepot and cups, and Longarm and Gray waited until the man had poured the thick black brew and left before continuing with their conversation. Longarm took a sip of the coffee and said, "Could still use a dollop of Maryland rye in it."

"Probably still using the same grounds as last night," said Gray. "Anyway, Long, you're a fellow lawman, and I could use a hand. There are six of those hombres, remember, and five of them are cold-blooded killers."

Longarm frowned in thought. He didn't like Sheriff Ed Gray, not even a little bit, and didn't much trust him, either. And Billy Vail might not like it if Longarm's return to Denver was delayed for what he might consider an unreasonable amount of time. On the other hand, Vail had always said that his deputies ought to cooperate with the local law as long as it didn't interfere with their own duties.

Longarm didn't have any duties at the moment, since the man he had come to pick up was dead. He was leaning toward accepting the sheriff's offer. . . .

When Gray said, "Besides, there's bound to be some damned good bounty money to split up when we bring in the corpses of those bastards."

Chapter 6

That decides it, Longarm thought grimly.

"Aim to bring 'em in dead, huh?" he said.

Gray shrugged. "I've never had a corpse try to escape. And I don't believe in taking chances with killers." He leaned forward and crossed his arms on the table. "How about it, Long? Are you in or out?"

"I'll ride with you," said Longarm. "I'll just have to send a wire off to my boss letting him know I'll be a few days later getting back to Denver."

"That's fine," Gray said with a nod. "Glad we understand each other." He grinned at the waiter, who was approaching with a platter piled high with food. "Now we can enjoy our breakfast."

"You don't seem to be in any big hurry to get on the trail of those hombres."

"They've been on the loose for several days already. Another hour won't make any difference one way or the other."

Longarm knew Gray was probably right about that, so he dug into the food with gusto. Brawling before breakfast *did* work up an appetite, not to mention the more pleasurable exercise he'd had earlier with Becky.

As he ate, Longarm thought about how he might be letting his dislike for Gray get him into a damned mess. He had no reason to feel any sympathy for the escaped prisoners Gray

45

was going to be hunting; on the contrary, Longarm had ventilated his share of fugitives who didn't want to face justice.

But he had never just gunned them down in cold blood, and he had a hunch that was what Gray aimed to do if he caught up with these men. Murder rubbed Longarm the wrong way, even when it was committed by a man with a badge. Hell, *especially* when it was committed by a man with a badge. By riding along with the posse, he could at least try to keep Gray from killing the prisoners unless it was necessary.

When they were finished eating, Gray lit up a cigar. Longarm scratched a lucifer into life and set fire to one of his own cheroots. Gray blew out a cloud of smoke and said, "We're going to have to see about a horse for you."

"And a saddle and tack. I usually bring my old McClellan along with me, but I didn't think I'd be horsebacking any on this job."

The sheriff grunted. "I don't know if we can come up with one of them army saddles or not."

"I can go out to the post and get a horse from their remount stock. Gear, too."

Gray shook his head and said, "No need to bother Stilwell with that. You said you'd done some cowboying. You ought to still be able to sit a stock saddle."

"I reckon. Think the livery stable will stake me to a horse?"

"I know it," Gray replied with a grin. "I own the place. I figure two dollars a day ought to be a fair price. You can turn in an expense voucher to your office for the rental, can't you?"

Right then, Longarm almost said the hell with it. That northbound train would be coming through in a couple of hours. Gray could handle his own snake stomping. But he thought about what the sheriff had said earlier about the bounty on corpses, and he reined in his temper.

"Two dollars a day will be fine." *Even if I have to pay it out of my own pocket.*

• • •

They had to pass the sheriff's office and jail to reach the livery stable, and Dewey was waiting on the porch. "Do I start rounding up the posse now, Sheriff?" he asked eagerly.

"Yeah, you do that," said Gray.

"How many men do you want to ride with us?"

"Fifteen or twenty ought to do it, counting Lloyd and Steve. But you're not going, Dewey."

The deputy looked stricken. "Not going?" he yelped like a kicked dog. "But, Sheriff—"

"I need you here, to look after things while I'm gone. You don't think I'd trust that job to just anybody, do you?"

Dewey blinked a couple of times and said, "Oh. Well, I reckon that's true. . . ."

"Of course it is. You round up the fellas, tell 'em to meet me at the livery stable with their horses, their guns, plenty of ammunition, and rations for a week."

"Yes, sir." Dewey hustled off again.

"That youngster's got more enthusiasm than I thought he did yesterday," said Longarm. "Looked like he was about to doze off while he was reading the *Police Gazette*."

Gray puffed on his cigar, took it out of his mouth, spat flakes of tobacco off his tongue. "He's an idiot. Only reason I keep him around is because his uncle's the county judge."

He should have expected as much, thought Longarm. Gray had some sort of angle for everything.

They walked on to the livery stable, where Longarm picked out a good-looking blood bay gelding as his mount. The horse was part of the sheriff's personal string, Gray explained as he congratulated Longarm on his choice. "A fine animal," the sheriff said.

"Too good to rent for two dollars a day?"

Gray shrugged again. "A deal's a deal."

Over the next half hour, the posse gathered at the stable as Dewey spread the word through town. They were a typical bunch, Longarm thought as he studied them: a few cowboys who were probably riding the chuck line, otherwise they wouldn't have been in town on a weekday; some of the town loafers, tired of playing dominos and forty-two and looking

47

for a little excitement; a couple of storekeepers, drawn no doubt by the promise of a reward of some sort; a gambler in a fancy frock coat; and two more men who wore badges. Gray introduced them to Longarm as his other deputies, Steve Karnes and Lloyd Hartley.

"Pleased to meet you, gents," Longarm said with a nod.

"You're the fella who tore up that hotel room this mornin', ain't you?" asked Karnes.

"I had a mite of help," Longarm replied.

Hartley chuckled. "Yeah, heard tell you went waltzin' with Sergeant Mike. I figured he'd come after me one night after I walked Miss Becky home from a dance, but he never did."

Karnes dug an elbow into his fellow deputy's ribs and snickered. "You done more than walk her home, and you know it."

"Well, so have you!" Hartley shot back.

Longarm sighed. He was starting to wonder if any of the grown men in this town *hadn't* shared Becky's favors. And she had looked so innocent, too.

Gray called the posse together. "Listen, boys, these are desperate men we're going after. Coldblooded killers, each and every one of them."

That wasn't strictly true, thought Longarm. Only five of the escaped prisoners had been convicted of murder. The telegram from the El Paso sheriff hadn't said why the sixth one had been going to prison. But Longarm figured Gray didn't want him to point that out right now.

"So you'd damned well better shoot them before they get a chance to shoot you," continued Gray, "or we'll be packing you back face down over your saddle."

The members of the posse nodded in understanding. None of them looked as if they had any trouble with the idea of bringing in the prisoners dead instead of alive. Dewey stood to one side, looking proud that he had assembled such a co-operative group.

"No telling how long we'll be out," Gray went on. "If we need more supplies or fresh horses, we'll commandeer them from the closest ranch we can find."

More nods. These citizens knew what to expect of their sheriff.

"All right, reckon I'd better swear you in." Gray lifted his right hand. "Hold up your hands. Do you swear to act as lawful deputies of Pecos County and follow the orders of the sheriff of Pecos County?"

The posse members called out their agreement.

"You're all sworn in, then," said Gray. "That makes it official." He turned toward his horse. "Mount up."

Longarm gripped the horn of his borrowed saddle and swung up onto the bay's back. He hadn't thought to ask Gray if the two dollars a day included the rent of the saddle, too. He supposed it did, but knowing the sheriff as he already did, Longarm thought it would be a good idea to confirm that as soon as he got a chance, before he ran up an even larger livery bill for Billy Vail to complain about.

The posse rode out of Fort Stockton, heading west, and as Longarm glanced back over his shoulder, he saw Dewey standing alone in the middle of the street, watching them go.

With Dewey holding down the fort, Longarm hoped the settlement would still be there when they got back.

Five days earlier

"I can't go any farther!" Ginny moaned as she sat down abruptly on the sand.

Myra turned toward the prostitute with a sneer on her face. "What's the matter, whore? Is this more work than letting a bunch of drunk cowboys ride you instead of their horses?"

Ginny started to struggle to her feet, saying angrily, "You no-good bitch—"

Abigail put a hand on her shoulder to stop her from getting up. "Just sit down," she said. "We could all use a rest." She looked at Myra as if daring the young redhead to challenge her statement.

Myra just shrugged. She sank down cross-legged on the hot sand, the chains clanking loudly in the desert silence.

She supposed Abigail was right. They were all tired. Exhausted was more like it. They had walked all the rest of the

49

day after fate had set them free from the prison wagon, rested that night, walked all the next day, slept again—or tried to sleep, since they were all in such pain from blisters and sore muscles that relaxing was almost impossible—then started walking again that day. It would have been easier to travel at night, out of the heat of the day, but Myra and Bridget didn't know this part of the country as well as they pretended they did. They didn't want to chance getting lost.

In the past forty-eight hours, all they'd had to eat was a stringy jackrabbit Myra had downed with one shot from the hip when the critter burst out of a clump of mesquite in front of them. The shot had been pure luck, but Myra had looked back at the others with an expression of smug confidence, as if she could perform such feats of sharpshooting all day long without breaking a sweat. She'd skinned the rabbit with her knife, and they had eaten it raw, since they had no way to start a fire. All the others except Bridget had started to balk at eating uncooked rabbit, but when they saw that they wouldn't get anything if they were too finicky, they had overcome their revulsion and joined in the meal.

That had been almost twenty-four hours earlier, though, and everyone was hungry again. Weak from hunger, in fact, and sunburned and sore to boot. At least they didn't have to worry about drinking water. Diablo Creek ran all the way into the Davis Mountains, which was their destination. The stream had shrunk to a trickle, but it was steady and didn't seem to be in any danger of drying up. The water was muddy and didn't taste very good, but no one complained about that.

In the whole time since they had left the prison wagon, they hadn't seen a single human being.

Timothea brought that up now. She said to Myra, "I thought you said there were ranches down this way."

"There are. We just haven't got to any of them yet."

"Do you know when we will?" asked Deborah.

Myra shrugged. "We'll get there when we get there."

Bridget suddenly gripped her arm and pointed. "Look yonder, honey."

Myra looked and saw a thin tendril of gray smoke rising

50

into the blue sky. It was coming from a valley in the foothills of the mountains, which appeared to be about five miles away. Of course, the mountains had looked like they were five miles away since the middle of the day before, but Myra knew they had to be getting close. They just had to be.

Otherwise, she wasn't sure how long she could keep this bunch going. All of them were city girls except her and Bridget, and they didn't know a blasted thing about surviving out here on the frontier.

Myra scrambled to her feet, the links of the chain clinking again. "That smoke's got to be coming from a ranch," she said. "Come on. We can be there before the afternoon's over. Good water, hot food, maybe some way to get these chains off us."

"Why would whoever lives on that ranch want to help the likes of us?" asked Ginny.

Myra put her hand on the butt of the Colt she had taken from the driver of the prison wagon. "I don't intend to give 'em any choice."

Reuben Wood's dog started barking just as the shadows of dusk were gathering. Reuben was in his cabin fixing some supper when he heard the old hound. Immediately, he took the pan of bacon off the stove and went to the wall where his pa's old Henry rifle hung on a couple of pegs. The Henry was loaded, of course. Reuben's pa had taught him that an unloaded gun was as worthless as a pair of tits on a boar hog. He worked the rifle's lever to jack a shell into the chamber and strode to the doorway. The door stood open to let in the cool breeze that usually sprang up in the evenings.

"What's the matter, boy?" Reuben called to the hound, who stood in the open area between the two sections of the cabin known as the dogtrot. The other side was empty. Reuben figured he and his wife would use it as a bedroom for their kids, once they got around to having kids . . . and once he found some woman who was willing to marry him and move out here to this ranch on the ass end of nowhere, of course.

The hound just looked off into the dusk toward the barn

51

and kept baying. Reuben squinted. He didn't see anything moving around out there, but that didn't mean much. Timber wolves sometimes came down into the foothills from the mountains, and they were hard to see. So were Apaches, though in the two years that Reuben had lived alone on the ranch, no Apaches had come raiding. They were all across the border now in Mexico, or so he'd heard.

But you never could tell, so he tightened his grip on the Henry rifle and walked quickly toward the barn. Wolves or Apaches, either one, they weren't going to get his horses.

He used the barrel of the rifle to push open one side of the barn doors and then stepped back quickly, leveling the weapon at the shadows within. "I got a gun out here," he called, "and I know how to use it. You best come on out now, whoever you are." Wolves wouldn't understand English, of course, and 'paches probably wouldn't, either, but it made him feel better to holler out like that.

Then the young woman stepped out of the shadows of the barn, and Reuben's eyes almost bulged right out of his head. She had hair like the setting sun, and she was the prettiest thing he had seen in a month of Sundays.

She had a gun in her hand, too. Reuben saw it as her hand came up out of the folds of her dress, and then the muzzle of the gun bloomed with fire even brighter than the young woman's hair. As the impact of the bullet knocked Reuben back into the dark, he tried to hang on to that brightness.

But it slipped away from him, and so did everything else.

Chapter 7

"Damn it, you didn't have to shoot him!" Ginny cried as she rushed forward out of the barn.

"He had a gun!" protested Myra. "He said so himself. And right there it is." She gestured at the Henry rifle lying beside the fallen man. "What was I supposed to do, let him shoot us?"

"He wouldn't have shot us," said Abigail. "We're women."

"When he saw these chains, there's no telling what he might have done."

Ginny dropped to her knees beside the rancher, who was balding despite his relative youth. He had a short beard and blood down the left half of his face from where the bullet had plowed a furrow on the side of his head just above the left eye.

"Besides," Myra went on, "I only grazed him. He ain't dead, is he?"

"No," said Ginny. "He's breathing, and his pulse is pretty good."

"See?" That was the second fancy shot in a row that Myra had made, but she had to wonder if this one was all that lucky. She'd been aiming to kill the rancher.

"I wonder if anyone else is here," said Abigail.

"Probably just that old hound," said Bridget. The animal

was still in the dogtrot, baying at them. "Anybody else would have come running at that shot."

"Well, we'd better go check inside the cabin anyway. Bridget, get the rifle," ordered Myra.

Ginny asked, "Hadn't we better tend to this man's wound?"

"You can fuss over him later. Right now I want to make sure nobody else is around."

Reluctantly, Ginny went with the other women. She looked back over her shoulder at the wounded rancher as she shuffled toward the cabin.

Neither of the cabin's two sides were very big, and one of them was completely empty. It took only a few minutes to convince Myra that they were indeed alone here on this isolated ranch, except for the unconscious man lying in front of the barn. They returned to him, and Myra said, "All right, let's take him inside. All of you except Bridget, grab hold of him."

"Why doesn't she have to help?" asked Ginny. "Because she's your girlfriend?"

"Because we've got the guns. Our job is to watch out for trouble."

Abigail said, "Let's just pick him up. I'm tired of this squabbling."

The four women stooped and took hold of the rancher, each of them taking an arm or a leg. With grunts of effort, they picked him up. He was heavier than he looked. They carried him into the side of the cabin where he obviously lived and placed him on a narrow bunk covered with a threadbare blanket.

A bucket of water stood on the rough-hewn table in the center of the room. Ginny lifted her dress, ripped a piece from the hem of the cotton shift she wore underneath the prison garb, and dipped the cloth into the water. Then she took it and began swabbing away the blood from around the wound. Despite the care she took to be gentle, the rancher let out a moan of pain even though he didn't wake up. Ginny shot a hostile glance toward Myra.

54

Myra did her best to ignore the soiled dove. "I saw a chisel and a sledgehammer out there in the barn," she said. "I reckon we can use them to bust these chains off of us."

"And there are plenty of good horses in the corral," added Bridget. She hefted the Henry. "We've got this rifle now, too."

Suddenly, the rancher began to thrash around. "Somebody give me a hand with him," Ginny called. "He's out of his head!"

Abigail and Deborah both went over to the bunk and leaned down to grip the rancher's shoulders. Ginny hovered over him and said urgently, "Take it easy, mister. You're all right now. Just settle down."

She had to repeat the words a few times before they seemed to penetrate the man's stunned brain. Finally his struggles subsided, and he lay back on the bunk and gave a loud groan. "What the hell happened to me?" he asked. He stared wide-eyed up at Ginny and added, "Oh, Lord, I've died and done gone to heaven!"

That comment brought a snort of contempt from Myra. Ginny had heard such sentiments before, of course, from the men who had paid her to lie with them. They all meant it about as much as she did when she told them they were different, that she really felt something with them. But this man's words seemed to be genuine. Ginny smiled down at him and laid the damp cloth over his forehead. "Just rest now," she told him. "You've been shot, but you'll be all right."

"Shot!" the rancher repeated, and he started up again. He would have sat up had it not been for Abigail and Deborah holding him down. "I remember now! Some redheaded gal shot me!"

"I just creased you," said Myra. "Consider yourself lucky, mister."

He twisted his head to look at her, saw her standing there with her hand on the butt of the Colt and Bridget beside her holding the Henry rifle, and he said, "Lord, what's all this? Women with guns?"

"Take it easy," Ginny told him again. "You won't help anything by getting all worked up."

Timothea chose that moment to move slightly, and the chain connecting her ankle to Deborah's clanked. The noise was loud inside the close confines of the cabin. The rancher turned his head again and looked down at the floor. His eyes bulged even more as he saw the chains connecting the six women who stood around his bed.

"What . . . what are you?" he struggled to ask. "Convicts?"

"That's right, mister," snapped Myra. "So don't think it'll bother us one little bit if we have to shoot you again."

"Nobody's shooting anybody," Ginny insisted.

"As long as you behave and do what you're told," added Myra to the rancher.

The man moaned again. "My head hurts too damned bad for this to be some sort o' crazy dream. You're really here, aren't you? All six of you?"

"That's right," said Ginny. "We're real. But we don't want to hurt you."

"We just want to get these chains off," said Abigail.

"And some horses," added Bridget.

Myra said, "And all the guns and ammunition you've got."

For a long moment, the rancher made no response. Then, abruptly, he started to laugh. The noise must have hurt his head, because he winced, but he kept laughing anyway.

"What the hell's so funny?" Myra demanded angrily.

"I . . . I been thinkin' lately," said the rancher, "that I got to get me a woman out here. Now, who shows up on my doorstep out o' nowhere but six gals, and they're all pretty, too! Only thing is, they shoot me and want to rob me blind!" He howled with laughter.

"Shut up!" yelled Myra. She jerked the gun from its holster. "Shut up, you crazy fool!"

Ginny moved quickly, putting herself between Myra and the rancher. "Leave him alone!" she said. "Haven't you done enough to him already?"

Myra looped her thumb over the hammer of the Colt, even

though it was a double-action and didn't need to be cocked before it could be fired. "Back off, whore," she began, "or I'll—"

"Stop it!" screamed Timothea. "Both of you, just stop it!"

None of the others expected such a violent reaction from her. They stared at her in surprise and amazement as she went on in a loud voice. "I've had all I can take of this! I've lost my husband, I've been sent to jail, I've nearly drowned. . . ." She slumped onto the floor and began to sob. "I just want it all to stop. I wish none of it was real."

"Oh, it's real, all right, honey," Bridget said quietly. "Sometimes I wish it wasn't, too."

Myra shot her a wounded look, but before the redhead could say anything, Abigail spoke up again. "Why don't we all just settle down?" she said reasonably. "I see a pan of bacon over there that's half-cooked. I don't know about the rest of you, but I'm famished."

"So am I," said Deborah.

The rancher lifted a hand and said weakly, "Help yourself, ladies."

Ginny smiled at him again. "Thanks, mister."

"Name's Reuben. Reuben Wood."

"I'm Ginny."

"Mighty pleased . . . to meet you, Miss Ginny."

"Save that for later," said Myra. "Let's finish frying up that mess of bacon and see if we can find something else. That won't be enough for all of us."

Abigail quickly took charge of the cooking, aided by her sister. Deborah found the makings for flapjack batter and stirred up a batch. Soon the smell of food cooking filled the cabin again, making the mouths of the women water.

Timothea stopped her sniffling and found some china plates in a cabinet. "They were my mama's," Reuben Wood said from the bunk. "She got 'em when her and my pa got married, back in Georgia."

"Before the war," guessed Ginny.

Reuben nodded. "Yes'm."

"My folks came from Georgia, too." She had thought she

57

heard traces of a familiar accent in his soft drawl. She dabbed at the bullet crease on the side of his head with the damp cloth. "You have any whiskey here?"

"Yes, ma'am, there's a bottle in that trunk over there."

Ginny went to fetch it, stepping carefully so as to avoid tangling the chains. All of the women were moving around the cabin as if in the steps of an intricate dance. That was the only way to keep from getting hopelessly tangled up.

Ginny found the half-full bottle of whiskey. She pulled the cork stopper and dribbled a little of the fiery stuff over Reuben's wound. He grimaced at the pain. "Burns even more on the outside than it does on the inside," he managed to say through gritted teeth.

"It'll ease up," Ginny assured him. Her fingers explored the area around the wound. She was no expert on bullet creases, but she didn't think any damage had been done to his skull. The only injury seemed to be the raw scrape along the side of his head. "You want a drink of this?"

"No, ma'am," said Reuben. "I don't hold with drinkin' 'cept on special occasions."

From across the room, Myra asked, "What would you call getting shot?"

"Pure bad luck?"

Ginny said, "That's enough talking. You just rest now." She waited until Reuben had settled back on the bunk and closed his eyes, then she stood up and moved over to the table.

"If you treated all your customers that nice," said Myra, "you must've been the most popular whore in El Paso."

Ginny thought about telling Myra what she could go and do to herself, but then she thought it probably wouldn't be anything new for the redhead. Instead she just looked back over at Reuben. His eyelids flickered a little, but she couldn't tell if he was awake or not. Nor had she been able to tell if he had heard either of the times when Myra called her a whore. By this time in her life, it really shouldn't have bothered her, she told herself.

But sometimes it did. Sometimes it sure did.

•   •   •

Despite the ache in his head, Reuben was able to sit up and eat some of the flapjacks and bacon and drink a cup of coffee. He felt better after he had eaten. "Been a long time since I had a woman-cooked meal," he said to Ginny. "Always seems to taste better somehow than the grub I rustle up for myself. Thank you, ladies."

Abigail and Deborah, who had done most of the cooking, both smiled. "You're welcome," said Abigail.

Myra said, "It's been a while since you two fixed supper for anybody, hasn't it? And the last fella who ate your cooking got his head beaten in with a singletree, I recall."

The sisters glared at her. "You don't know how to leave anything alone, do you?" Deborah asked angrily.

"I just want Reuben here to know what kind of gals he's got visiting him," said Myra. "We're all killers, mister, except for that fuzzy-haired Miss Priss over there." She pointed at Timothea, who flushed with a mixture of anger and embarrassment. "She's just a swindler."

Reuben glanced at Ginny, as if he found it hard to believe that she could possibly be a murderess.

Myra laughed. "She's a killer *and* a whore. Bridget and me, we're cattle rustlers, but we shot some cowboys the last time we tried to wideloop a herd. And like I said, those other two beat the older one's husband to death."

Reuben looked at her intently, his expression not so much frightened as it was sad. "Why are you tellin' me all this?" he asked.

"So you'll know the kind of woman you're dealing with, mister."

"I get the idea. You're a bunch of female desperadoes."

"It's not as bad as it sounds, Reuben," Ginny said quickly. "Really, it's not."

The rancher shrugged. "Hell, I don't care what you've done in the past. My pa shot a couple of carpetbaggers before we lit out of Georgia after the war. I always figured they had it comin' to 'em." He shook his head. "I don't know if any of the fellas you killed deserved it or not, but what's done is done."

"Glad to hear you're taking such a reasonable attitude," said Myra. "Now, what about these chains?"

"You can bust 'em off with a chisel and my sledgehammer, like you said earlier. Or if you want to wait until in the mornin', I'll give you a hand gettin' 'em off."

Ginny said, "You won't be in any shape to help us, not with that head wound."

"This little scratch?" Reuben touched the injury gingerly and winced. "Shoot, I've been kicked in the head by a mule. A little bullet crease ain't nothin'."

"Well, if you're sure . . ."

Reuben looked around at the women. "You got my word on it, ladies. I'll get them chains off you, first thing in the mornin'."

Myra hesitated. She hated to wait any longer to rid herself of the chains, but on the other hand, they couldn't travel in the dark anyway. A few more hours of being chained together wouldn't hurt anything.

"All right," she said. "But don't you try anything funny during the night." An idea occurred to Myra, and she went on, "In fact, just to make sure you don't, I reckon one of us ought to sleep in that bunk with you. That way you won't be able to get up and sneak around." She looked at Ginny. "You're elected, since you're on the end of the chain."

Myra was hoping to embarrass Ginny with the suggestion, but she realized a moment later that she had failed miserably. Ginny smiled and said, "I'll be glad to share Reuben's bunk . . . if he'll have me."

Reuben blushed furiously. "I . . . I reckon that'd be all right. Under the circumstances and all."

The bunk was narrow. Ginny slid onto it and had to snuggle closely against Reuben's side to keep from falling off. "How's this?"

"Uh . . . uh . . . just fine, ma'am."

Ginny rested her head on his shoulder. "One of you blow out the lamp when you get ready," she said sleepily.

Myra rolled her eyes, and Bridget said, "Ain't you the little matchmaker?"

"Shut up. Get some blankets and spread them out, so at least we won't have to sleep on bare floor."

"It'll be better than the ground," said Abigail.

"A lot better," added Timothea.

A few minutes later, Abigail blew out the lamp, and darkness settled down inside the cabin. Reuben dozed off quickly, and soon his snores filled the air. The others had more trouble sleeping.

Ginny didn't mind. It had been a long time since she had spent an entire night with a man, she thought. Most of her customers hadn't been willing to pay for more than an hour, and many were even quicker than that. She found herself enjoying the sensation of lying next to Reuben: his warmth, the steady rhythm of his breathing, the feel of his muscles under the woolen shirt. There would be something to be said, she decided, for experiencing this every night for the rest of her life.

Unfortunately, when morning came, Reuben would bust the chains off them, and then they would have to be on their way again, running from the law. Ginny knew she would never again be able to remain in one place for very long.

Or would she?

Chapter 8

The loud ringing of sledgehammer, chisel, and anvil filled the barn the next morning. Heat had already started to build, even though it was still early in the day, and sweat had soaked through Reuben's shirt in places. The bandage that was tied around his head was damp with perspiration, too. He paused to catch his breath before lifting the hammer to strike another blow. He wasn't quite as strong as he had thought he would be, but he didn't want to let Ginny see that.

She had volunteered to go first. Her foot was propped up on the anvil. Myra was holding the chisel, and before Reuben had ever swung the hammer for the first time, she had said to Bridget, "If he tries anything, shoot him."

Bridget, who was holding the Henry rifle, had just nodded in understanding.

But so far, the blows struck by Reuben had been on target. Even so, the impact of steel against steel had to be passing painfully through the shackle into Ginny's ankle. She kept her face set in tight, stoic lines.

With the muscles in his shoulders bunching, Reuben lifted the hammer for a fourth stroke. The heavy head fell, and this time, Ginny gasped. But the shackle sprang open, revealing the raw sores it had rubbed on her skin over the past few days. She lowered her foot from the anvil and tried to step back, but her legs gave way under her.

Reuben was at her side an instant after she fell. "Are you all right, Miss Ginny?" he asked anxiously.

"Yeah, I . . . I will be," she said. "It feels good to finally get that damned thing off me."

Reuben looked down at her ankle. "I've got some liniment that'll do them sore places a world of good."

Myra said, "Fetch it later." She handed the chisel to Bridget and then drew the Colt. "First you finish busting loose these shackles. And don't forget, I'll be watching you mighty close."

Reuben straightened slowly and went over to pick up the sledgehammer he had dropped when he sprang to Ginny's side. "I don't reckon I'm likely to forget, Miss Myra," he said heavily. "Not with you wavin' that gun in my face."

"Just get busy," snapped Myra, and a moment later the ringing of the hammer sounded again.

It took nearly an hour to break loose all the shackles, and by the time he was finished, Reuben was exhausted. The women weren't in much better shape. All of them were grateful, however, to be free again, able to move any way they wanted without having to worry about tripping over the chains or jerking the shackles against raw skin. Reuben got the jar of liniment from the tack room in the barn, and even though all of them knew it was what he used on the horses, they were thankful for its soothing coolness as he spread it on their ankles.

Reuben lingered the longest over Ginny, and Myra felt an unaccountable surge of jealousy as she watched the tender way he ministered to the soiled dove. "That's enough," she said.

Ginny and Reuben ignored her. Ginny placed her fingers on the rancher's wrist and said, "Thank you, Reuben. I'm surely glad we ran across your place."

"Me, too, ma'am. Even if I did get shot."

Myra shook her head in disgust. "Come on. I want to get out of here."

"Go if you want," Ginny said as Reuben helped her to her feet. "I'm staying right here."

That declaration took the rest of the women by surprise.

They stared at her, and Myra said, "What do you mean by that?"

"Just what I said." Ginny faced them defiantly. "I'm staying here with Reuben."

"You mean that, Miss Ginny?" he said, looking as dumbfounded as the rest. Hope suddenly shone in his eyes.

She turned to him and smiled. "I sure do."

"This is crazy!" exclaimed Myra.

"I think it's sweet," said Abigail, and Deborah added, "I do, too."

"But you're on the run from the law," Bridget protested. "You can't just stay here."

"Why not?" asked Ginny. "The chains are off now. We can all go wherever we want."

"No!" said Myra. "We have to stick together. Otherwise the law will catch us for sure."

Ginny shook her head. "You're wrong. We'll each have a better chance if we split up. Of course, I can understand why you and your little friend would want to stay together," she added, unable to resist the gibe.

"Look, it's over," said Timothea. "Like Ginny said, we can do what we want now that the chains are off. I don't mind staying with Myra and Bridget for now, until we get to a town somewhere. I can't set off across this wasteland by myself. But once we're back in civilization . . ."

"That's right," put in Abigail. "I think the rest of us should stick together for now, but if Ginny wants to stay here, I don't see anything wrong with that."

Ginny moved closer to Reuben, linked her arm with his. He beamed down at her. "I reckon we could go down to Fort Davis in a few weeks when the circuit preacher comes through and have him make everything legal, if that's all right with you."

"You . . . you want me to be your wife?"

"Why, sure."

"Don't you think somebody's going to wonder where your bride came from?" asked Myra. "You're fools, damned fools. If she shows her face in a town with you, it won't be a week before the sheriff rides up to arrest her, and you, too, for hiding her out.''

"No, ma'am," said Reuben. "I'll just tell folks that Miss Ginny here is my fiancée from back in Georgia, come out here at last to join me. I don't reckon anybody'll have any reason not to believe that."

"Not until somebody spots her picture on a reward dodger," Myra said with a sneer. "All right, go ahead, if that's what you want, but I still think you're a couple of blasted lunatics." She turned sharply and limped off toward the house.

Tears burned in her eyes as she did so, though she blinked them away rapidly and wouldn't have admitted their presence to anyone to save her life. She was crying because of the sheer lack of gratitude on Ginny's part, Myra told herself. After all, it was she who had gotten them out of that prison wagon and she who had kept them moving across the burning sands when everybody else wanted to just sit down and give up. If it wasn't for her, they might all be dead by now, she thought.

And what did Ginny do? Why, just run out on the rest of them the first time some *man* smiled at her and did something halfway nice!

"I got plans, big plans," Myra muttered to herself, "and if that high-and-mighty whore don't want to be part of them, it's her damn loss!"

An hour later, five women mounted horses in the open space between the cabin and the barn. Timothea's horse was wearing an old saddle, but the others would have to ride bareback for now. As the least experienced rider, Timothea got the saddle.

She and Abigail and Deborah were now wearing simple dresses that had belonged to Reuben's mother, and Myra and Bridget were clad in trousers and shirts taken from the old trunk in the cabin. They had found a battered felt hat that had once belonged to Reuben's father, and Bridget had appropriated it. Myra had taken the Confederate army cap that had been worn by the elder Wood during the War Between the States and tucked up her long red hair underneath it. She still wore the holstered Colt, but Bridget was no longer carrying the Henry. Reuben had talked her into leaving it behind, over Myra's objections, and had instead given Bridget a double-barreled shotgun that didn't have the sentimental value of the Henry. Myra had wanted to take all the guns and ammunition on the place, as well as all the horses, but the rest of the women had overruled her.

"Fine bunch of fugitives y'all are," grumbled Myra. "Letting the fella you're stealing from decide what you can steal!"

"Reuben's been good to us, even though he got shot and all," said Bridget. "We can't leave him and Ginny out here with no way to defend themselves and no way to get around."

"It was her own damn choice!"

"So it was," said Abigail, "but we have to be reasonable."

Being reasonable, thought Myra, ought to mean the rest of them doing what she damned well told them to do, but they didn't seem to see it that way. So she nodded and went along with what they decided . . . for now.

"So long, Ginny," Bridget said from horseback. "You're sure you don't want to go with us?"

"I'm sure," said Ginny as she hugged Reuben's arm more tightly.

"Good luck to you," said Abigail, and Deborah echoed, "Good luck."

Timothea smiled and said primly, "I hope the two of you are very happy together."

"Oh, hell!" spat Myra. "Can we get out of here?" She dug her heels into the flanks of her horse and sent it leaping into motion.

The others called their farewells and rode after her. They had been gone for several seconds, with Ginny and Reuben watching the mounted figures dwindling in the distance, before Ginny said, "They're going north, not south."

"Now, that's funny," Reuben said with a frown. "That's the direction you came from. Wonder why they're going back that way?"

The other women had noticed the direction Myra was leading them, too, and Bridget moved her horse up alongside her friend's mount. "Myra!" she called over the pounding of hooves. "Where in blazes are we going?"

"If we're going to spend the rest of our lives on the run, it's not going to be for something as penny-ante as rustling some cows and shooting a couple of punchers!" Myra turned her head to look at Bridget, and her eyes were on fire. "We're gonna go rob us a bank!"

Diablo Creek

Longarm reined in as Sheriff Ed Gray lifted a hand to bring the posse to a halt. They were on the eastern bank of a small stream that meandered through the rugged West Texas wasteland between several ranges of hills and mountains. A bridge had once crossed the creek at this point, but nothing was left of it but a few pilings.

"Bridge must've washed out a couple of weeks ago after those big rains up north of here," said Gray. He leaned over and spat onto the dusty road. "The prison wagon wouldn't have been able to get across here if the creek was still up."

"Where would they go?" asked Longarm.

"There's a ford a ways south of here," Deputy Steve Karnes said.

Gray nodded. "Springer's Ford. That's likely where the driver would have headed if he didn't want to wait for the creek to go down." He heeled his horse into motion, walking it out into the now-shallow stream. "Come on."

This was the posse's second day after leaving Fort Stockton. It had taken this long just to reach the area where the prisoners had escaped. No one knew exactly when the incident had occurred, but it had probably been over a week since the killers had freed themselves. Picking up their trail might not be as difficult as it sounded, however, since there had been no rain and little wind during that time. Tracks tended to last quite a while under those conditions, and a man with a keen eye could follow them.

Despite his dislike for Ed Gray, Longarm had to admit that the sheriff could read sign. As the posse crossed the creek and rode up onto the western bank, Gray pointed to some barely discernible tracks on the hard ground. "Wagon wheels," he grunted. "And they're headed south, just like we thought."

The posse followed the tracks for a couple of miles to a place where the streambed widened and flattened out even more. "Springer's Ford?" Longarm guessed.

Gray nodded as he reined in. "Yep. You can see where the wagon went into the water."

Longarm studied the tracks and agreed with Gray's statement. The ruts of the wagon wheels were more visible here because they had been formed in soft, muddy ground that had been baked hard by the sun in the intervening days. Longarm looked downstream and saw in the distance where the creek entered a narrow canyon that slashed through a range of low hills. "If the creek was up and they got washed into that canyon, no telling what happened to them," he said.

"Let's go take a look," suggested Gray.

They couldn't follow the stream through the canyon; the walls were too sheer and came right down to the water. But Gray knew a trail that led over the hills, and a half hour later the posse rode down a gentle slope onto a long, sandy flat next to the creek. Some good-sized mountains rose in the distance to the south, and Longarm knew they had to be the Davis Mountains. He had been to Fort Davis a time or two before, but not lately.

"Son of a bitch!" Lloyd Hartley suddenly exclaimed. "Look yonder, Sheriff!" He pointed to a little knoll on the eastern side of the creek.

Longarm had already seen it, his attention drawn by the sun glinting off some bit of metal over there. The corpse was sprawled facedown on the side of the knoll, its head lower than its feet.

"Must be either the driver or the guard," said Gray as he spurred ahead.

Once again the posse crossed the shallow stream. Gray dismounted and rolled the body over. Longarm grimaced as he saw what was left of the man's face. It wasn't much. Buzzards and coyotes had been at him, and Longarm was a little surprised the predators hadn't dragged the man's remains off.

"Looks like he might've had a beard," commented Gray. "Probably old Pete Sessums. He drove the prison wagon sometimes for the sheriff over in El Paso County." He turned to his deputies. "Steve, Lloyd, you ride on downstream a ways, see what else you can find, while some of the other boys dig a grave for this poor bastard."

The deputies nodded and galloped off. Gray "volunteered" several members of the posse to serve as a burial detail, then called Longarm over to his side.

"Hard to tell what killed Pete," he said in a low voice.

"I didn't see any bullet wounds," commented Longarm.

"Neither did I, but like I said, it's hard to be sure when a fella's been so gnawed on. I'm going to put down in my report that he was killed by those escaped prisoners, though."

"For all you know, he drowned," Longarm pointed out.

"Maybe, but I say he was murdered."

Longarm knew what Gray was getting at. If the prisoners were blamed for killing the guard and the driver, it would look even better when Gray brought them in dead.

"Put down whatever you want, Sheriff," said Longarm. "This is your show." If Gray wanted him to approve of the lie, then the sheriff was going to be disappointed. Not that Longarm hadn't shaded the truth a little on some of his own reports in the past. He just figured that he'd had a damned good reason to do so on those occasions, and that Sheriff Gray didn't on this one.

"Sure, Long," Gray said, seemingly affable. His eyes were hard, though, and Longarm knew the sheriff was going to be watching him closely for any signs of trouble.

Longarm lit a cheroot and leaned his head toward the south. "Your boys are coming back," he said.

Sure enough, Karnes and Hartley rode up a minute later. "The other fella is about half a mile downstream, Sheriff," said Karnes. "He's even more chewed up than this one, but you can still tell that somebody stove his head in."

Gray shot a look at Longarm, as if to confirm that he had been right to blame the prisoners.

Hartley added, "There's a couple of mule carcasses down

70

there, too, and Lord, they stink to high heaven!''

"Any sign of the wagon itself?'' asked Gray.

Both deputies shook their heads. "No telling how far downstream it floated,'' said Karnes.

Longarm took his cheroot from his mouth and used it to point at something none of the others seemed to have noticed. "There are some footprints along the bank here.''

Gray swung around and said, "So there are.'' He knelt beside the tracks, studying them intently, and the frown on his face deepened as he did so. "These were made by folks wearing shoes, not boots.''

"They're sort of small, too,'' Longarm pointed out.

Gray looked up at him sharply and exclaimed, "Hell, if I didn't know better, I'd say these tracks were made by—''

"Women,'' Longarm finished.

Chapter 9

"What the hell would *women* be doing 'way out here the hell and gone from anywhere?" said Gray.

Longarm shook his head. "I don't know, Sheriff, but I reckon it's like the old hymn says."

"Hymn? What hymn?"

Longarm pointed to the south, in the direction that the tracks led. "Further along we'll know more about it."

Gray's face was taut and angry, and he looked for all the world like he wanted to yank his hat off, toss it on the ground, stomp it good, and cuss for a while. Longarm knew the feeling, having experienced it a time or two himself. But finally the sheriff just nodded and turned his attention to the burial detail. "Don't you have that grave dug yet?" he demanded.

"Gettin' there, Sheriff," said one of the men assigned to the grim task of scooping out a grave. They were all drenched with sweat from the hot sun beating down on their efforts.

"Steve, ride down to where that other body is and dab a loop on it," Gray instructed Karnes. "Drag it back up here so we can bury it along with this one. I don't want to take the time to dig another hole."

Karnes looked dubious. "Ain't much left of the fella but bones, Sheriff. If I go to dragging the corpse over that rough ground, it's liable to fall apart."

"Do the best you can," snapped Gray. "The poor bastards

73

are long past caring, anyway. Don't know why we're even bothering to bury 'em.''

Karnes shrugged and turned his horse. He motioned for Hartley to come along with him, and the two deputies rode off downstream.

Gray looked at the tracks and said again, "Women."

"Beats all, don't it?" Longarm commented dryly.

"You think that prison wagon was full of women?"

It was Longarm's turn to shrug. "I don't see any other tracks around here. I suppose the women could've come along later, after the prisoners took off."

"Then what happened to their tracks?"

"Blown away by the wind?"

Gray shook his head. "It hasn't been that windy." He rubbed a hand over his face. "Damn, this makes things more complicated."

Longarm knew what he meant. Folks wouldn't be as disposed to just accept whatever story Gray told if he brought in the corpses of six women. He might have to take them alive, rather than dead.

Karnes and Hartley returned a few minutes later with the grisly remains of the other man. The corpse was largely intact, Longarm noted, and he figured the deputies must have been pretty careful with it. Both bodies were lowered into the shallow grave that had been scooped out in the side of the knoll. The posse members covered them over with dirt, then built a primitive cairn of rocks over the grave. Gray watched impatiently, and he grew even more restless when one of the townies insisted on saying a prayer. When the posse was finally ready to go again, Gray swung up into the saddle and called, "Come on!" He heeled his horse into a fast trot as he followed the creek bank, his eyes on the footprints left by the mysterious pilgrims.

Longarm rode directly behind the sheriff, keeping a close eye on the tracks himself.

Two miles downstream, the posse found the prison wagon itself, or rather, what was left of it. It had been battered against some rocks in the middle of the creek until it had come apart.

Nothing was left except some wagon wheels and other debris scattered along the bank of the stream, but Longarm, Gray, and the others could tell that it had once been the vehicle they sought.

Longarm mentally pieced together the most likely scenario to explain everything the posse had found. The bridge had been washed out by the flooding, rain-swollen creek. The prison wagon had come along, and rather than wait for the stream to go down, the driver had chosen to go south to Springer's Ford. But the normally safe crossing had proven dangerous, and the wagon had been washed away by the swift current and carried into that narrow canyon.

While that was going on, the prisoners had somehow gotten free. Longarm had no idea whether they had actually killed the driver and the guard, or if the two men had met their deaths by misadventure, as the coroners liked to phrase it. The prisoners had headed south, and judging by the tracks they left, they were either women or gents with really small feet. Longarm was betting on women.

He had noticed something else, too. The corpse that Gray had tentatively identified as belonging to Pete Sessums, the wagon driver, had not been wearing a gunbelt. Longarm seriously doubted that any man would start across West Texas at the reins of a prison wagon full of killers without packing iron, even with a well-armed guard along. That meant something had happened to the driver's gun, and Longarm had a pretty good idea what it was.

Those gals likely had it, and given their history, they probably wouldn't hesitate to use it.

Longarm felt a peculiar but familiar prickling on the back of his neck. Not knowing if the feeling was prompted by the thoughts going through his brain or if his instincts were actually trying to warn him, he turned his head and looked back. Just for a second, he caught a glimpse of movement on a hill several miles behind the posse. Not many men could have even seen whatever it was, but Longarm's eyes had been trained by years of experience to notice such things. *Probably a rider,* he thought.

But why would anyone be on their back trail? Longarm couldn't think of a reason.

Unless maybe the hunters had become the hunted.

Longarm didn't seen anything more of whoever had been following them. The posse was still a good ways north of the Davis Mountains when Gray called a halt for the night. "It'll be a cold camp tonight, boys," he said. "Don't want those fugitives seeing our fire. It's bad enough they might have spotted the dust we kicked up today."

And so might the Apaches, if that gent on their back trail was of that persuasion, thought Longarm. Not long before, most of the Mescaleros and Eastern Chiricahuas had withdrawn into northern Mexico after losing a battle with U.S. Army troops at a waterhole called Tinaja de las Palmas. There was no telling when some of them might get it into their heads to come raiding again, though. Gray's idea not to build a fire was a good one, even though the posse would have to make do for supper with jerky, hardtack, and water instead of beans and coffee.

The campsite was a small rise topped with a few scrubby mesquite trees and prickly pear cactus. Several men tended to the horses, hobbling them since there was no way to rig a corral. Others, including Karnes and Hartley, took their rifles and stood guard duty. Longarm knew he would be taking a turn later in the night.

He hadn't said anything to Gray about the rider behind them in the distance. For that matter, Longarm couldn't be sure what he had seen was really a man on horseback. It could've been a deer or a coyote, he supposed. It was even within the realm of possibility that his eyes had played a trick on him and he hadn't really seen anything at all, but he didn't think that was very likely.

A white man following the posse more than likely wouldn't push on after dark, reasoned Longarm. Apaches might, but the sheriff had already posted guards, so there wasn't much else that could be done. Longarm felt confident that the sentries wouldn't fall asleep on the job; they had been glancing around too nervously at the vast, rugged, lonely landscape for that to be very likely.

So Longarm didn't waste any time or energy worrying overmuch as he gnawed on jerky and hardtack and washed down the grub with swallows of water from his canteen. He had a definite craving for a cheroot, but he didn't indulge it. On more than one dark night in the past, he had lined his gunsights on the glowing red eye of a quirly that some poor gent just hadn't been able to resist smoking. Longarm didn't intend to die in the same foolish fashion.

A couple of days of riding had left Longarm tired. He fell asleep almost immediately when he rolled himself in his borrowed soogans, and slept soundly until somebody put a hand on his shoulder. Then he was instantly awake, and even though he didn't seem to have moved, his fingers were wrapped around the butt of his Colt.

"Come on, Long," said Sheriff Gray. "Our turn to stand watch."

Longarm stood up and put on his hat. He took the Winchester that Gray handed him. Even with only a thin slice of moon riding in the sky, the night was fairly bright from the illumination of thousands of stars. Longarm had noted on previous visits to West Texas that those stars always seemed brighter and closer out there than they did almost anywhere else.

A chilly breeze was blowing. The heat of the day had long since seeped away. The air would be cool now until morning. Longarm stretched, tucked the rifle under his left arm, and followed Gray a short distance from the camp. The soles of their boots crunched quietly on the sand and rock underfoot.

"What made you become a lawman, Long?" Gray asked, taking Longarm by surprise with the question.

Longarm frowned a little. "Don't rightly remember," he said. "I just sort of drifted into it, I reckon you could say, and I was good enough at it that I stuck with it. Now I'm too blamed old to do anything else."

"That's not true. You're still a young man. You could start over . . . especially if you had a wad of cash to help give you that start."

Longarm's jaw tightened, and he said, "A wad of cash is sort of hard to come by on a deputy marshal's wages."

"Yeah, but toting a badge sometimes puts you in a position where you can add a little something to those wages."

The son of a bitch still hadn't given up on corrupting him, thought Longarm. Gray was bound and determined that every lawman had to be as morally bankrupt as he was. Longarm didn't want to feel self-righteous, but he had a strong urge to clout the bastard in the chops.

"I ain't no snowy-fleeced lamb," he said coldly, "but I try to stay on the right side of the law. That's what Uncle Sam pays me for."

"You're supposed to be a smart man. Once I thought about it, I recollected that I've heard of you. You're the one they call Longarm. You've got quite a rep."

"Not for stealing."

"Nobody said anything about stealing," argued Gray. "Are you saying a man's a thief just because he doesn't pass up an opportunity to make a little money?"

"I'm not saying anything," replied Longarm, tiring of this discussion. "But if we're standing here jawing at each other, we can't very well be looking and listening for anybody who's trying to sneak up on the camp, now can we?"

Gray grunted angrily. "Have it your way, Long. I've tried to figure you out, and I'm tired of butting my head against a rock wall. You don't have any jurisdiction in this case, so you're just a member of the posse like anybody else. Stay out of my way, and we'll leave it at that, all right?"

For a silver dollar, Longarm would have gotten on his rented horse the next morning and ridden back to Fort Stockton, leaving Gray and the rest of the posse to chase down those killers. But nobody was likely to offer him a silver dollar, he thought, and besides, the situation had changed. There was at least a chance the fugitives were women, and Longarm knew he couldn't ride away and leave them to Gray's mercy, such as it was.

"I'll try not to tangle my twine with yours, Sheriff," he said.

Gray stalked off into the darkness, apparently satisfied with Longarm's answer. Longarm's hands tightened on the Winchester as he fought down his own anger. He and Gray were like two locomotives racing at each other on the same track. If nothing happened to divert one or the other of them, sooner or later there was going to be one hell of a crash.

The night passed quietly. The posse members rolled out of their blankets before first light, and by the time dawn was graying the sky in the east, they had eaten breakfast and saddled their horses. A short while later, the sun popped up over the horizon like a giant orange-red ball bounced by a kid. Longarm, Gray, and the other members of the posse rode south, still following the stream.

"Diablo Creek runs all the way into the Davis Mountains," commented Gray. "Looks like that's where the folks we're after are headed."

Longarm nodded in agreement. "More than likely. I've been looking at those tracks, and I've noticed something else."

"What's that?" Gray's attitude was still somewhat surly this morning, but he wasn't going to pass up an opportunity to learn something that might prove to be important later on.

"Look at those scrape marks between the sets of footprints," Longarm said, pointing at the ground next to where he and the sheriff rode.

"They're dragging something along the ground between them," Gray said after a moment. He checked the other tracks. "They're all like that. What in blazes—?"

"Chains," said Longarm. "They're chained together, ankle to ankle, I'd say. That pretty much confirms that the fugitives we're after are women, all right."

Gray rubbed his beard-stubbled jaw. "Yeah," he said slowly. "A chain gang full of women. That's not what I figured we were going after when we left Fort Stockton."

"I don't reckon any of us thought that—" Longarm began. He stopped short and reined in, his eyes narrowing as he peered ahead of them at a long ridge that ran at an angle toward the creek. The ridge was topped by a litter of boulders and cactus, and for a second Longarm would have sworn that he saw the sun reflecting off something up there that was metal. . . .

That thought passed through his brain in an instant, and in the next heartbeat he was launching himself out of his saddle, shouting to Gray and the rest of the posse, ''Ambush!''

Chapter 10

The town of Van Horn, two days earlier

No amount of talk would persuade Myra that she was crazy. She was bound and determined to rob a bank.

"The law's already after us," she had said the night before as they sat around a cold camp and gnawed on some of the biscuits they had brought from Reuben Wood's ranch. "To stay ahead of those damned badge-toters, we're going to need good horses, more guns, and plenty of food and ammunition. Those things cost money. And the best place to get money is out of a bank."

"You've forgotten one thing," Abigail had pointed out. "None of us are bank robbers. We don't know how to go about it."

Myra had snorted in disgust. "How hard can it be to walk into a bank, wave a gun under the nose of some pasty-faced clerk, and tell him to give us all the money?"

"What if somebody shoots at us?" Deborah had asked.

"We shoot back at 'em, for God's sake!"

Abigail, Deborah, and Timothea had all shaken their heads. Timothea summed up their feelings by saying dubiously, "I just don't know. . . ."

"We can do it," Bridget had put in. "I know we can, Myra."

"Of course we can, honey. You just ride along with me, and everything'll be fine, just fine."

Of course, Myra had said the same sort of thing months earlier when she had come up with the idea of her and Bridget being cattle rustlers, and that scheme had landed them behind bars facing a life sentence. Bridget didn't point that out, however.

Myra knew she had to get the others to go along with her plan. Otherwise, the whole group would fall apart and she would have no hope of keeping them together. Why it was important that she do so, she couldn't have said. All she knew was that it had hurt bad enough when Ginny abandoned them, and Myra hadn't even *liked* Ginny.

They had already given her trouble about riding north instead of south. That was heading right toward any lawmen who might be looking for them, they had argued. But Myra had veered northwestward, pointing out that any pursuit would likely begin where the prison wagon had wrecked on Diablo Creek and follow the stream south toward the mountains. The trail Myra followed ran a good ten miles west of the creek. "Nobody's going to be looking for us in these parts," she had argued in favor of doubling back. "They'll all be south of here."

The others couldn't beat that logic, but that didn't mean they weren't still trying. In a rare show of rebelliousness, Bridget had even said, "Seems to me like we ought to be heading for Mexico."

"We can always make a run for the border later, after we're better outfitted and have plenty of money. We don't want to be broke south of the Rio Grande."

That was certainly true. So, the others had gradually fallen in line with her plans, and now they were riding into Van Horn, a bustling, fairly new town that hadn't even existed until the Texas & Pacific tracks had come through. It also had the only bank between Pecos and El Paso.

The five women drew some odd looks from the folks on the boardwalks of the town as they rode along the wide, dusty main street. Myra angled her horse toward a livery stable, and the others followed. An old man with leathery skin and bowed legs, most likely a stove-up cowboy who'd had to give up his riding job, came out of the barn and looked at them curiously as they reined their mounts to a halt and dismounted.

"Howdy, ladies," he said to them. "Somethin' I can do for you?"

Myra inclined her head toward the horses. "Thought you might like to do a little horse-trading. We need some fresh mounts and four saddles."

The old man gave her a long look before he switched his gaze to the horses. Myra was uncomfortably aware of how her breasts pushed against the shirt she wore and the way her hips filled out the denim trousers. She was glad when the old man squinted at the horses and rubbed his jaw in thought.

"Looks like fair-to-middlin' animals," he said after a minute, "but I couldn't swap you even up for anything better'n what you already got. And if I was to throw in saddles and tack for four of 'em, I'd sure have to have somethin' else to boot."

"How much?" Myra asked tightly.

The old man moved his lips and wrote in the air with a gnarled finger as he calculated. "Say . . . a hunnerd dollars?"

"Fifty," said Myra. She patted the shoulder of the horse she had been riding. "These are damn fine mounts."

"Fair-to-middlin'," the old man said again. "Seventy-five."

"Sixty."

The old man's sharp chin, which bristled with a few white hairs, jerked in a nod. "Done."

"Get the fresh horses saddled and ready," Myra told him. "We'll be back in a bit to fetch them."

"All right, ladies." He licked his lips as he watched them go.

"Now what?" asked Bridget in a quiet voice as they stepped up onto the boardwalk on one side of the street.

"We've got another stop to make before we visit the bank," replied Myra. She led the way into a cavernous, high-ceilinged general store. There were a handful of women inside, possibly the only respectable women who lived in the whole town, which was still pretty raw. They gave the five newcomers looks of mingled distaste and curiosity.

A bald man with a spade beard wore an apron and stood behind a counter in the rear of the store. He was the only person in the building other than the female customers. He gave Myra and her companions a smile and said, "Good day to you, ladies. May I help you?"

"We need to buy some guns and ammunition," Myra told him. The man's bushy eyebrows arched upward in surprise. She added, "And some damned chewing tobacco."

That brought the reaction she hoped for from the town women. They all sniffed in disgust at Myra's crudity, and one of them said in haughty tones, "We'll come back and finish our shopping later, Mr. Canfield."

"But ladies—" the storekeeper began to protest. It was too late. The other women swept out of the store.

That was exactly what Myra wanted. Now they were alone in the store with the storekeeper. He turned back toward them with an angry look that vanished as he found himself staring into the barrel of the pistol Myra held. Fear replaced the anger.

"My God!" he sputtered. "See here! What . . . what do you mean by this outrage—"

"Shut up!" Myra hissed. Without taking her eyes off the storekeeper, she flung an order over her shoulder. "Bridget, watch the front door. Let me know if anybody's headed this way."

"Right," Bridget said as she hurried back toward the front of the building.

"Abby, Debbie, grab that roll of twine off the counter and tie this gent up good and proper. Thea, find something we can use to gag him. Move quick now, we ain't got much time."

Canfield found his tongue again. "Young woman, you can't do this—"

Again Myra interrupted him. "Shut up, I said! If you want to give us trouble, I'll just blow your brains out, mister. It don't matter a damn to me either way."

Canfield paled and swallowed hard. He put his hands behind

his back as Abigail and Deborah tied his wrists together. Then, following Myra's orders, he sat down behind the counter and allowed the two women to bind his ankles. Timothea stuffed a balled-up rag in his mouth and tied it in place with a brightly-colored bandanna she picked up from a stack on the counter.

"Turn the sign around on the door and shut it," Myra called to Bridget, who did as she was told. To the others, Myra said, "Get into some better riding clothes. There's plenty of shirts and trousers and boots in here. Bridget and I will start gathering guns and cartridges and supplies."

The looting of the store proceeded quickly and efficiently. In less than a quarter of an hour, Abigail, Deborah, and Timothea were dressed much as Myra and Bridget were in range clothes. All five of the women were now wearing holstered Colts and wide-brimmed hats, except for Myra, who still sported the Confederate cap she had worn from Reuben Wood's ranch. They shrugged into long dusters meant for men. The bottoms of the coats brushed the floor around their feet, but the dusters would help to conceal their sex. They took Winchesters from a rack behind the counter and stuffed boxes of .44-40 cartridges into the pockets of the dusters.

"You know, this is almost exciting," said Deborah. "I'm actually starting to feel like an outlaw."

"I'd just as soon not get used to the feeling," said Abigail. "But I guess if we're going to be on the run from the law anyway, we might as well do it right."

Timothea said worriedly, "They send you to jail longer for robbing a bank than they do for trying to swindle someone, don't they?"

"If you want to turn yourself in," Myra said in a hard voice, "nobody'll stop you. But you'll have to wait until after we're gone. Better remember, though, you've already escaped from that prison wagon and helped rob this store. They'll tack on a few more years to your sentence just for those things."

"But none of that was my fault!"

Myra snorted. "You reckon the law's going to pay any attention to that?"

85

Timothea sighed and said, "No, I suppose not." She squared her shoulders. "Well, let's get on with it."

"That's the spirit," Myra said with a nod. "Come on. Let's go rob us a bank."

They left the storekeeper tied up behind the counter, closing the door behind them and locking it with a key they had taken from his pocket. If anyone passing by on the street thought that was unusual, none of them raised any uproar about it. Indeed, no one seemed to pay much attention to them. Despite its small size, Van Horn was a busy place, and being on the railroad line as it was, strangers probably came and went all the time without the townspeople giving them a second thought.

That was all about to change, thought Myra. Soon, everybody would pay attention to them. They would be famous from one end of Texas to the other if she had her way about it.

The First Cattlemen's and Merchant's Bank was up ahead, a squatty adobe building that wasn't anywhere nearly as impressive as its name made the establishment sound. Several horses were tied at a double-hitch rack in front of the bank. Myra hoped there weren't too many customers inside the place.

Her bootheels rang on the wide planks of the boardwalk as she and the other four women approached the door of the bank. Myra grasped the latch, turned it, stepped inside. The thick adobe walls made the interior of the bank cool and dim. It took Myra's eyes a few seconds to adjust after the brightness of the day outside.

When she could see clearly, though, she saw that there were four men inside the bank: a teller in a cage behind the counter, a man sitting at a desk off to one side, and a couple of customers in front of the teller's window. The man at the desk glanced up curiously at the newcomers, and so did one of the customers. The other man was only paying attention to the money the teller was counting out into his hand.

Bridget kicked the door shut behind her, and Myra brought

up the Winchester she'd been holding down beside her thigh, partially concealed by the folds of the duster. "Hands up, gents!" she called in a loud voice that rang with authority. "This is a holdup!"

She hoped like hell that Abigail, Deborah, and Timothea were backing her play.

"You heard what she said." That was Abigail, believe it or not. "Get those hands up."

The four men were all startled. The clerk and the customer he had been waiting on complied with the order, raising their hands shoulder high. The man at the desk came to his feet, his knuckles resting on the desktop as he said angrily, "See here, what's the meaning of this?"

But the fourth man, who was dressed like a cattleman, smiled cockily and said, "Why don't you little ladies run on back to your knittin'? Robbin' banks is man's work."

And as soon as he had said that, he turned, drew his own pistol, and leveled it at the man behind the desk, saying, "I know all about what came in on the train, Keller. Better give it up if you don't want to wind up dead."

Chapter 11

Myra didn't know who was more astounded, she and her companions or the man behind the desk, who was probably the bank president. He had already been gaping at the spectacle of five women in men's clothing coming into his bank to rob it, and now his jaw dropped even more as he stared at the man with the gun.

"I . . . I don't know what you're talking about," he finally managed to say.

"Sure you do, Keller," the man said coolly. "A whole strongbox full of nice, fresh cash to stock this bank."

Myra liked the sound of that, but she didn't care for the way the rest of this hold-up was going. She said, "Hey!"

The other bank robber glanced lazily over his shoulder. He was a handsome devil, with blue eyes and clean-cut features and sandy blond hair that curled down the back of his neck under his hat. He smiled and said, "You gals still here?"

"Look out!" Deborah suddenly yelled.

The man twisted, saw the other customer yanking a gun from behind his belt. "You're nothin' but a damned thief, Durrell!" the man shouted as he tried to bring his weapon to bear.

The man called Durrell pivoted smoothly and fired, all in the same motion. The slug took the customer in the chest and flung him back against the teller's window. He dropped his gun and pitched forward on his face, the breast of his shirt already bloody.

"Cover the teller!" snapped Myra. She turned her own rifle toward the bank president, who had yanked open a drawer in his desk and was pawing around inside it, no doubt for a gun. Myra said, "Don't!"

Keller froze, staring bug-eyed at the barrel of the Winchester in Myra's hands. That gave Durrell the opportunity to lean across the desk and slash him across the face with the butt of the gun, which he had deftly reversed in his hand. Keller sagged backward and moaned, blood rolling down his face from the gash Durrell's blow opened up.

Durrell flipped the gun around so that it was again pointing at Keller. "That shot'll draw flies," he said. "Quick now, Keller. Where's that strongbox? I know it came in on this morning's train."

"No, it didn't," Keller practically moaned. "The reserve bank in El Paso was late getting the shipment together. It won't be here for four days yet. It's the truth, I swear it, Durrell!"

The man called Durrell didn't look quite so handsome now as desperation settled on his face. Myra thought the bank president was telling the truth. A glance at the wet spot spreading on the crotch of his trousers showed how terrified he was. He was much too scared to be telling anything but the truth.

"Damn it!" snapped Durrell. He looked over his shoulder at Myra and the other four women. "Get out of here," he told them. "Out the back, hurry!"

"Wait a minute," began Myra. "We came to get money—"

"There's nothing here but petty cash. Now git! There's no law here but a constable, but he'll come running any minute."

Myra knew the man was right. She was almost sick with disappointment, but she knew he was right. "Come on!" she said to the others as she ran past the bank president's desk toward the back door. She heard the footsteps of the others right behind her.

They burst out into the sunlight and turned left, back toward the livery. Suddenly a pair of gunshots sounded inside the bank. One of the others cried out in surprise and fear, but Myra didn't know which one. She glanced back and saw that none of them seemed to be hit. They kept running, holding the rifles crossways across their chests in front of them. There was no sign of the man called Durrell.

"What . . . are we . . . goin' to do now?" Bridget asked breathlessly as she came alongside Myra.

"Get back to the stable . . . and get the hell out of here!" That was all they could do now, thought Myra. She grimaced, and not just from the effort of running in riding boots. Of all the banks in Texas, she had chosen one to rob that didn't have enough money on hand to make it worthwhile. Not only that, but another bandit had even gotten there ahead of them!

She wondered fleetingly about Durrell. He had known the bank president, and Keller had known him. Obviously a local. Had he come to Van Horn strictly to rob the bank?

And what was that about a strongbox full of money coming in on a train four days from now?

Myra knew she couldn't worry about that now. She had to concentrate on getting herself and the others out of Van Horn safely. She swung around a corner into an alley, turning so sharply that she stumbled slightly. Behind her, Timothea almost fell—would have had it not been for Bridget grabbing her arm to steady her.

They were next to the livery stable, just as Myra had thought. When they reached the street, she turned toward the big double doors and ran into the old hostler, who was going the other direction. The old man yelped and flew backward, landing hard on his rump. Dust puffed in the air from the street.

Myra reined herself in. "Where are those horses?" she demanded.

The old man opened and closed his mouth a couple of times, but no sound came out. Myra stuck the muzzle of the Winchester in his face. He said, "Don't shoot me! They're right there in the corral!"

Bridget had already seen the fresh, saddled mounts and was

swinging open the corral gate. "Come on," she said to the others.

A man across the street saw Myra pointing the rifle at the hostler and yelled, "Hey! What's going on over there?"

Myra swung the Winchester toward him and pulled the trigger. The rifle cracked sharply and the recoil nearly tore the weapon from her hand. Firing from the hip like that, the best she could do with the bullet was to knock a chunk out of a water trough a good fifteen feet from the man who had shouted, but that was close enough to send the man diving through an open doorway in the search for some cover.

The hostler grabbed at her leg. She kicked loose and swung the barrel of the rifle against the side of his head with a thud. The old man slumped over in the dust. Myra leaped past him and ran into the corral. Bridget, Abigail, and Deborah were already mounted, but Timothea was struggling to swing up into the saddle of one of the remaining horses. Myra put a hand on Timothea's bottom where the denim of the trousers was stretched tightly over it and pushed. Timothea settled down in the saddle with an "Oof!"

Myra grabbed the reins of the remaining horse and scrambled up on its back. "Let's go!" she called to the others as she dug the heels of her boots into the flanks of the skittish animal. The horse bolted out of the corral with Myra hanging on for dear life. The other four women thundered after her.

A lot of folks were on the street by now, especially to the east where the bank was located. Myra hauled on the reins of her mount and turned it toward the west, only to see riders coming from that direction. "Damn it!" she shouted. She twisted her head and looked to the north.

That way was no good, she realized bitterly. There was no dependable water in that direction short of Delaware Creek, and that was almost all the way up in New Mexico Territory. If they ran north with a posse on their heels, sooner or later thirst would force them to surrender just to save their lives.

That left south, the direction they had come from. Rugged country, but there was water to be had, and hiding places if they could reach the Davis Mountains. As the folks on foot to the east started running toward the five women, and the horsebackers to the west broke into a gallop, Myra shouted, "Hyyaaahh!" and dug in her heels once more. Her mount lunged ahead, pounded down a narrow alley between two buildings, and emerged onto the open plains south of Van Horn's single street. The horse leaped over the Texas & Pacific tracks and kept running. Myra looked back to see the other four women strung out behind her. Bridget was bringing up the rear, herding the others along like a mama hen with her chicks.

Puffs of smoke came from the town. People were shooting at them, Myra realized. Give them a few minutes, they'd round up a posse and ride in pursuit. So it was important that she and her companions put as much distance as possible between them and the settlement.

The taste of defeat was sour in Myra's mouth. Her plan had been a good one, she told herself. It wasn't her fault that it hadn't worked out. Just pure bad luck, that was what it was. If that bastard Durrell hadn't been in the bank when they came in, they would have gotten away with a little money, anyway.

On the other hand, if not for Durrell, they probably wouldn't have known about that strongbox coming in on the El Paso train four days from now. Myra was going to have to think about that, providing that they could get away from the folks who chased them from Van Horn. And providing, as well, that they didn't run into any lawmen who might already be looking for them because they had escaped from that prison wagon. If everything broke just right, they could still wind up rich and famous. Well, infamous, really, but that was just as good, thought Myra.

She clung to that hope, leaned forward in the saddle, and rode harder.

Back in Van Horn, confusion ruled. Folks rushed this way and that, saddling horses and talking about chasing those damned bank robbers, but they were waiting for someone to step forward and assume command. Inside the bank, grim-faced men stared at the bodies sprawled on the floor in pools of blood.

The local sawbones was working over the bank president, Herman Keller, who had been shot in the chest. The teller, Martin Jennings, was lying behind the counter, shot through the head. He was dead as could be. So was the man lying in front of the teller's window, a rancher named Culverhouse. He had been lying facedown when everyone rushed into the bank, drawn by the sound of the shots, but someone had rolled him over to reveal the big blood stain on his shirt. His eyes stared sightlessly at the ceiling.

"Step aside, step aside," ordered an authoritative voice, and the crowd around the bodies parted. A tall, sandy-haired man strode through the gap. As he loomed over the doctor and Keller, the bank president drew one last, desperately gasping breath as his eyes widened grotesquely. Then Keller's head lolled to the side and a ghastly rattle sounded in his throat.

The sawbones glanced up at the newcomer and said, "You're too late. Keller just died. Now he won't be able to tell us who did this."

"I've got a pretty good idea. Folks saw five people in dusters come in here not long before the shooting started, and five strangers took fresh horses from Patterson's Livery and rode off shooting. Women, believe it or not. I'll round up a posse and go after them."

"Women?" The doctor grunted in surprise. "If that don't beat all. Think you can catch them? We hired you to put a stop to such lawlessness, you know, Durrell."

Constable Pete Durrell nodded determinedly. "I'll catch them, all right. Those women are cold-blooded killers, and I'm not going to let them get away."

Myra looked back from time to time and saw the cloud of dust rising into the sky several miles behind them. That had to be the posse. She and the others had a good lead; the posse had been slow to get away from Van Horn for some reason. And the horses on which they rode were strong and fresh. They stood a good chance, Myra thought, of giving the slip to their pursuers.

They rode along dry arroyos, across rocky flats, choosing

the trails that wouldn't take tracks as easily. Nobody said much. Myra suspected that Abigail, Deborah, and Timothea were still pretty shaken from the violence back there in the settlement. Bridget was all right, though, cool as she could be. That came as no surprise to Myra. When those cowboys had been chasing them after the failed attempt to wideloop that herd of cattle, Bridget had kept her head just fine. She'd been calm as she fired back into the group of punchers, even when a couple of the cowboys went sailing out of their saddles.

If the other three hadn't been along, Myra would have been confident she and Bridget could get away without much trouble. She considered leaving them for the posse to find, but not too seriously and only for a moment.

They had come this far together, she told herself. They would stay together, no matter what came.

Except for that traitor, Ginny. . . .

Myra didn't call a halt to rest the horses until nearly sundown. By that time, the dust from the posse had fallen even farther behind them. Whoever was leading those men wasn't pushing them very hard, thought Myra. They weren't staying on the trail very well, either. The column of dust had veered back and forth several times during the afternoon, as if the posse had lost the trail for a while before finding it again. Myra guessed she was doing a good job in leading her group across places where they would be hard to follow.

The old hostler had put their canteens and supplies on the horses when he saddled them, and Myra was grateful for that. She dismounted, stretched, and untied her canteen from the saddlehorn to take a swig of water. The others followed suit.

"I never saw anyone shoot so fast as in that bank," said Bridget. "That fella Durrell must be a gunfighter."

"Oh, he wasn't that fast," scoffed Myra.

"You think you could shade him?"

Abigail laughed. "From what I saw, none of us could beat him with a gun."

"Maybe we'll just find out one of these days," said Myra, flushing. "He ruined our plan, and if we ever run into him again, I plan to settle the score with him."

95

Abigail's smile said plain as day she considered that big talk, nothing more. Myra got even angrier, but she reined in her temper. Fighting among themselves would just lead to more trouble.

The sun slipped below the western horizon, and night fell with the suddenness peculiar to this high desert country. After a few minutes, Myra swung up into the saddle. "Let's go," she said. "We're pushing on, even though it's dark."

"Are you sure that's a good idea?" asked Timothea.

"We'll have to go a little slower, but so will that posse, if they even keep moving. If they make camp for the night, we'll really get a lead on them."

No one could argue with that. They moved on into the night.

It was after midnight when the fugitives finally stopped and snatched a couple of hours of sleep. Neither they nor the horses could go on any longer. But Myra made sure they were up before dawn and moving again.

Today there was no telltale cloud of dust in the distance behind them. *They've given up and gone back to Van Horn,* thought Myra. Either that, or the posse was so far off the trail that there was no hope of them ever finding it again.

The women rode all that day, eating and drinking in the saddle. The Davis Mountains loomed up in front of them, but with the peculiarities of such terrain, the peaks didn't seem to come any closer no matter how far the women rode. They made an actual camp that night, though it was a cold one, with no telltale fire to give away their position, and then pushed on again the next morning.

An hour later, things were starting to look familiar.

"Damn," Myra grated to herself as she looked around at the landmarks.

"What's wrong?" asked Bridget from beside her.

"We're getting close to that ranch again. I think it's in those foothills up ahead."

"You mean Reuben's place?"

Myra nodded. "Yeah. I didn't mean to lead us back where

96

we came from. I was just trying to make sure we shook that posse from Van Horn.''

"What's wrong with going back to Reuben's ranch?'' asked Abigail. "I'm sure he and Ginny would be glad to see us. We could probably get some more supplies there, too.''

Myra turned her head and looked over her left shoulder, instinct making the skin on the back of her neck prickle. "That's what's wrong,'' she said, twisting in the saddle to point at a haze of dust in the air about a thousand yards away.

"That damned posse!'' exclaimed Bridget. "How could they have found us? I'd have sworn we lost them.''

"Maybe it's them,'' said Myra, "or maybe it's some other lawmen looking for us. Or it could be Apaches.''

"Apaches?'' Timothea repeated. "You mean savages?''

"They raid around here from time to time. Wasn't all that long ago it was worth a white man's hair to ride through these parts alone.'' Myra took off her Confederate cap, letting her red hair tumble loose around her shoulders, and used a sleeve to wipe sweat from her forehead. "Either way, we've got to see who that is and set up a little reception for them.'' She pointed toward a ridge with some brush and boulders along its crest. "Up there. That's where we'll wait. If it's not Indians, or anybody else looking for us, we'll let them ride on by.''

"If it's the law . . . ?'' said Bridget.

Myra lifted her Winchester. "We discourage 'em—with lead.''

"You mean shoot them,'' said Timothea. "Bushwhack them, isn't that what you'd call it?''

"Damn right,'' snapped Myra. "You got a better idea? Maybe we ought to just surrender.'' Her voice dripped scorn.

"Come on,'' said Abigail. "We can at least see who they are.''

The dust was closer now. Myra and the others rode quickly toward the ridge, crossing a stream she recognized as Diablo Creek along the way. They urged their horses up the slope, then reined in at the top. After they had all dismounted, Myra had Bridget take the reins and lead the horses down the far side of the ridge. "You're the only one I trust to hang on to them," said Myra. "The rest of you, come with me. Pick out good spots behind those rocks. If we have to do any shooting, we can hold this ridge against big odds."

But not indefinitely, she thought. Sooner or later, they would be picked off or overrun. But the others didn't have to know that.

The four women settled themselves behind some boulders and waited with their rifles pointed down the slope. Myra didn't have much confidence in the shooting skills of her companions, but this would be pretty easy, at least at first. If they threw enough lead, they'd empty some saddles, that was for sure.

The riders came into view. The men were too far away for their features to be plainly seen, but Myra could tell they were white, not Apaches. After a moment, she saw sunlight glinting on the badges worn by several of them. Lawmen, no doubt about that. And given the circumstances, there was no doubt about who they were searching for, either.

Myra took a deep breath and lined the sights of her Winchester on the barrel chest of one of the men who rode in the lead. The posse was close enough now so that she could see her target's craggy face. Suddenly, some instinct warned her that she ought to be more concerned with the other man in the forefront of the posse. She looked at him, saw a leaner, more rangy figure wearing a flat-crowned, snuff-brown Stetson. The brim of the hat shielded his face to a certain extent, but she could tell that he had sun-browned features and a longhorn mustache that curled out to both sides of his mouth. He rode with an easy grace.

Yeah. That was the man she needed to kill first.

She shifted the barrel of her rifle.

And the man in the brown Stetson piled out of his saddle, yelling a warning.

Myra cursed and jerked the trigger, making the Winchester buck heavily against her shoulder. She just didn't have any luck at all, she thought bitterly as she jacked the lever of the rifle and kept firing down into the posse.

Chapter 12

As he fell, Longarm palmed the Colt from the cross-draw rig. He landed heavily, but his hand was wrapped securely around the grip of the gun, so the impact didn't jolt it from his grasp. He rolled over, and as he did so a bullet slammed into the ground where he had just been, scattering dirt and rocks. The sharp crack of a Winchester sounded at the same instant.

More rifle shots rang out, all of them coming from the ridge. Longarm scrambled to his feet as he heard one of the posse members cry out in pain. He grabbed with his free hand for the reins of the bay, which was dancing around skittishly. One of the possemen nearby said, "Shit!", and doubled over in the saddle, clutching at his midsection. Longarm knew the man was probably gutshot.

Sheriff Gray had jerked his Winchester from its scabbard attached to his saddle and began blazing away with it, directing his shots toward the top of the ridge. "Fight back!" he shouted at the other members of the posse. "Fight back, damn it!"

Longarm knew the range was too great for his Colt. But if he and some of the other men could get around behind that ridge and catch the bushwhackers in a crossfire, they might have a chance. . . .

He grabbed the saddlehorn, swung up onto the bay, heeled it into a run. He passed Deputies Karnes and Hartley and shouted at them, "Follow me! We'll catch 'em in a crossfire!"

He didn't know if the deputies understood him, or if they even heard what he had said. He didn't take the time to look back and see if they were coming with him, either.

Then he heard a strangled scream and glanced behind him to see Lloyd Hartley pitching out of the saddle, blood spurting from his bullet-torn throat. Something plucked at Longarm's shirt sleeve as he looked ahead of him again. He knew it was a slug passing close by him.

In the heat of battle, a man couldn't think about how close he was coming to death. A miss was as good as a mile, as the old saying went. Longarm threw a shot at the crest of the ridge, not expecting to hit anything. It was just to show that he still had his fangs.

More bullets spurted dust in the air around the racing hooves of Longarm's horse, but as he neared the end of the ridge, the angle wasn't as good for shooting at him. Longarm threw a glance at the posse, saw that it was in utter disarray. Several men were down, either dead or badly wounded. A couple of horses had been shot, too. Gray was trying to rally his men without much success as fire continued to rake them from the top of the ridge.

Longarm knew he could still turn the tide if he could get behind the ambushers. He pushed the bay across the sandy shoulder of the ridge. Karnes was still with him.

As he pulled the horse's head to the left, Longarm looked up the opposite slope of the ridge. He spotted a group of horses with a duster-clad figure holding their reins. He couldn't see the riflemen atop the ridge, but the sight of the one holding the horses told Longarm the bushwhackers weren't Apaches.

The gent hadn't spotted Longarm and Karnes yet, either. With all the shooting going on, Longarm hoped he and the deputy could get pretty close before they were noticed.

At least one of the gunnies atop the ridge had figured out what the lawmen were up to, however. Another duster-clad figure appeared, waving an arm toward Longarm and Karnes as they charged up the slope. The fella holding the horses kept a tight grip on the reins but brought his Winchester around and fired it one-handed. The bushwhacker on the crest of the ridge opened fire, too.

A bullet sizzled past Longarm's head. Karnes cried out behind him. Longarm glanced back to see the deputy clutching his chest and swaying in the saddle. That had been a damned lucky shot, but luck could kill a man just as dead as good aim. Karnes swayed too far to the side and tumbled off the horse. That left Longarm alone to carry the fight.

Well, not exactly alone, he realized a second later as more shots cracked from the far end of the ridge. A man on horseback was attacking the ambushers from that direction, too. One of the possemen must have gotten around there, thought Longarm.

He flung a shot toward the horses but couldn't tell if he hit anything. Then, a heartbeat later, his own mount faltered. The bay wasn't shot; it had simply stumbled as it lunged up the rock-littered slope. Longarm felt the horse falling and kicked his feet free of the stirrups. For the second time in less than five minutes, he threw himself clear of the saddle. *This is getting damned old,* he thought just before he slammed into the ground.

Again he rolled, coming to a stop on his stomach with his gun pointed up the hill. He aimed at the person holding the bushwhackers' horses and pulled the trigger. Nothing happened. Longarm cursed and looked at the Colt. It seemed to be all right, but he knew he must have hit it against a rock or something when he fell, jamming the cylinder.

Now he was in a fix.

The bay had fallen, but apparently it was unhurt since it lurched to its feet. Longarm scrambled up, too, and darted behind the horse, using it to shield him from the bushwhackers. The horse danced around, spooked by all the shooting, forcing Longarm to stay on the move if he wanted to keep the animal between him and the riflemen.

Meanwhile, the man who had attacked from the other end of the ridge was encountering heavy fire from one of the bushwhackers. His horse gave a sudden leap as a bullet burned along its shoulder, and the rider, unprepared for the reaction, went flying. He landed hard and rolled down the ridge, his

101

rifle slipping from his hands and skittering away on the rocky ground.

Longarm saw that and bit back a curse. From the limp way the hombre was sliding down the slope, the fall had knocked him unconscious at the very least. Longarm couldn't count on any more help from that direction. He fiddled urgently with his Colt, trying to unjam it.

There was no time for that, he saw a moment later. The two ambushers on this side of the ridge had mounted their horses and were galloping toward him. Longarm wished he had the little two-shot derringer he often carried in his vest pocket, but it was with the vest itself, rolled up in his saddlebag along with his suit coat and string tie. He had no way to defend himself, and by the time he could get back on his horse to make a run for it, the killers would be right on top of him.

They didn't plan to kill him, he realized a moment later. The riders drove Longarm's horse off to the side, then reined in and leveled their rifles at him. "Don't move, star-packer!" one of them called to him. "Get your hands up, you son of a bitch!"

The command was spoken in the clear, ringing tones of a woman's voice.

Longarm slowly raised his arms. The dusters worn by the riders were unbuttoned and gaped open enough for him to see that both of them had breasts poking out against the men's shirts they wore. One of the women was tall and slender, while the other was shorter and more abundantly endowed. The taller woman was the one who had spoken. She wore an old Confederate cap with crossed tin sabers on the gray felt above the stiff black bill. Her hair under the cap was bright red.

"Well, now," she said with a smile as she trained the Winchester on him, "what've we got here?"

"Deputy United States Marshal Custis Long," snapped Longarm. There was no point in trying to conceal his identity. If they searched him, as they were likely to do, they would find his badge and bona fides. Maybe knowing that they had bagged themselves a genuine federal lawman would make these two bloodthirsty women less likely to gun him down, he thought.

"Well, stand still and keep those hands up, Marshal," warned the redhead. "Bridget, go over there and check on the other one."

"What about the rest of the posse?" asked Bridget. She was the one who had been holding the horses. The three mounts she had turned loose were still bunched together fairly well on the slope of the ridge; rounding them up wouldn't be much trouble unless they decided to bolt.

The redhead snorted derisively in response to Bridget's question. "They turned tail and ran right after this fella tried to get around behind us. He was probably hoping to get us in a crossfire, but he didn't know his pards had already lit out."

Longarm knew it now, and his mouth tightened angrily at the news. Gray and the other survivors from the posse had fled, leaving him and Karnes on their own. Karnes was probably dead now, and Longarm was a prisoner. The other fella, the one Bridget went to check on, might be dead, too.

A moment later, it became clear that wasn't the case. Bridget dismounted and prodded the man in the side with a booted foot, and he stirred and groaned. "He's alive," she called to the redhead.

"Get him on his feet."

Bridget poked the man in the shoulder with the barrel of her rifle until he raised his head. With a shock, Longarm recognized him as Dewey, the young deputy Sheriff Gray had left behind back in Fort Stockton. *What in blazes is he doing out here?* Longarm asked himself, wondering at the same time if Dewey had been the mysterious rider he'd noticed on the posse's back trail. It seemed likely.

Under Bridget's goading, Dewey pulled himself shakily to his feet and stumbled over toward Longarm. He had a bloody scrape on the side of his face, suffered in the fall from his horse, but other than that and some general aches and pains and bruises, he seemed to be all right. "Where's Sheriff Gray, Marshal?" he asked as he came up to Longarm. "Is he all right?"

"He was the last time I saw him," replied Longarm. "Before he took off for the tall and uncut."

"I tried to pitch in and help when the shooting started,"

103

Dewey said miserably. "I've been trying to catch up with you and the sheriff for the past couple of days. Another telegram came in from El Paso." He glanced at their captors. "Seems the sheriff over there forgot to say anything in his first wire about how those escaped prisoners were . . . were women. I thought you and the sheriff ought to know."

"We sort of figured that out, old son," Longarm said dryly.

"But you didn't know that after they escaped they robbed the bank up in Van Horn and murdered three people."

From the corner of his eye, Longarm saw the redhead jerk slightly at the deputy's words, as if they had taken her by surprise. "That's enough talking," she said. "Get up that hill."

Dewey stumbled as he started up the slope. Longarm put a hand on his arm to steady him. The two women, Bridget and the redhead, walked their horses along behind. When they reached the crest, three more women were waiting for them. These three were dressed like Bridget and the redhead, in range clothes and long dusters. Two of them were blondes, and Longarm knew right away they were sisters. The other one had thick, curly brown hair that she tried to tuck under her hat, but it kept straying out. All the women carried Winchesters.

"Six of you escaped from that prison wagon," commented Longarm. "What happened to the other one?"

"She's dead," snapped the redhead.

Longarm sensed there was more to the story than that, but he figured the redhead wasn't in much of a mood to tell it. Nor did he particularly care at the moment. He didn't like being ambushed, not even by gals as pretty as these.

From up here on top of the ridge, he could see the trail where the posse had been riding before the shooting broke out. He saw Lloyd Hartley's body lying sprawled on the ground. A dark pool of blood around the deputy's head was being soaked up fairly quickly into the thirsty sand. On the other side of the ridge, the body of Steve Karnes was visible, too. But to his surprise, Longarm didn't see any other corpses.

"It's a damn good thing we weren't depending on the three of you to bring down those possemen," the redhead said sharply to the others. "I never saw such piss-poor shots in my life."

The older of the blonde sisters said, "Deborah and I were seamstresses, not assassins."

"I never fired a rifle before in my life," said the one with curly hair.

And these are the hardcases who'd busted out of that prison wagon? thought Longarm. Bridget and the redhead seemed to still have some of the bark on them, but the others, despite their rough garb, looked like they ought to be in a drawing room somewhere sipping tea.

"Well, we're just lucky I was able to bring down a couple of them and wound a few more," said the redhead. "You kept an eye out after they ran off to make sure they weren't going to double back, like I told you?"

The older blonde pointed to a distant smear of dust in the sky. "That's where they went, and they took the wounded men with them. That should slow them down even more if they come after us again."

Longarm spoke up, saying, "They'll come after you, all right. Sheriff Gray's not going to give up that easy." Not with the bounty that would be on the heads of these women, he added to himself.

"Sheriff Ed Gray, from Fort Stockton?" asked the redhead.

"That's right," Dewey said, trying to put a defiant tone in his voice. "And you'll be sorry you ever crossed his trail, lady."

"Hell, I'm sorry already. I've heard of Gray. He's supposed to be as crooked as a dog's hind leg."

"That's not true!" yelped Dewey. "He's a great lawman."

Longarm wouldn't have gone nearly that far; he figured the redhead's opinion of Ed Gray was a lot closer to the truth than Dewey's hero-worshipping view. But at the moment he was much more concerned with what this odd bunch of female outlaws planned to do with him and the deputy.

He wasn't the only one worried about that. The older blonde pointed the barrel of her rifle at Longarm and Dewey, making

105

Longarm narrow his eyes a little, and asked, "What are we going to do with them, Myra?"

So the redhead's name was Myra. It suited her, thought Longarm. She looked at them and said, "They're hostages, in case that posse or some other bunch gets us in a tight spot. We've got us a couple of tin stars to hide behind."

Longarm laughed grimly and said, "I wouldn't count overmuch on that, ma'am. Sheriff Gray would hesitate maybe a second before sacrificing us if it meant getting to you. Maybe."

Myra's lip curled as she looked at him. "You saying we ought to go ahead and shoot the two of you now, lawman?"

"Nope. I'm saying you ought to let us go, maybe even surrender to us. It'll go a lot easier on all of you if you do."

It was Myra's turn to laugh. "Sure, and wind up at the end of a hang rope."

"Texas hardly ever hangs women," said Dewey, "no matter what they've done."

Myra ignored him and turned her horse south. "Mount up," she said to the others. "We've flapped our jaws long enough. You two, get on your horses. Try anything and I'll gun you down. Count on it."

Longarm didn't doubt her for a second. He had seen the way she picked off Steve Karnes, and from what she had said earlier, he guessed she was the one who had killed Lloyd Hartley, too. In fact, she'd made it sound if she was the only one who had inflicted any real damage on the posse.

He wondered if that was true, or if she was just trying to protect the others from more murder charges when they were eventually caught by the law. Why would she care enough about them to do that?

Answering that question would have to wait, Longarm decided, because he had a more important one to ponder.

How in hell was he going to get himself and Dewey out of this mess?

Chapter 13

Bridget caught the horses Longarm and Dewey had been riding and led them over so that the two lawmen could mount
up. The other women had rounded up their horses, too. Myra
put Longarm and Dewey in the center of the group as they
started south toward the foothills of the Davis Mountains. She
took the lead and told Bridget and the curly-haired one, whose
name was Timothea, to bring up the rear. The blonde sisters
flanked the prisoners. The older one, Abigail, went to the right,
while Deborah, the younger one, took the left.

"Surrounded by beauty," Longarm commented with a grin.
True, he and Dewey were in a bad spot, but that didn't mean
he couldn't still appreciate the sight of a pretty gal.

"Shut up," Myra snapped over her shoulder. "Shut your
filthy mouth."

"Is it just me you don't like, honey, or all men?" drawled
Longarm.

Myra reined in and hipped around in the saddle, bringing
up her rifle as she turned. Longarm's jaw tightened involuntarily. He hadn't really meant anything by his flip comment,
but for a second he thought it was going to get him ventilated
anyway.

Then with a visible effort, Myra controlled her temper and
said, "Just be quiet, Marshal. If I want your opinion I'll ask
for it."

"Sure," Longarm said curtly. "But I'm getting a mite tired of having guns pointed at me."

"Get used to it," Myra threw over her shoulder as she heeled her horse into motion again.

They rode until midday, Myra setting a fast pace, and that brought them out of the barren flats and into the foothills. The air seemed cooler and more comfortable right away when they entered a valley between pine- and cedar-covered slopes.

Longarm spotted some smoke off to the east that was probably coming from the chimney of a ranch house. Myra led the group away from the smoke, though, heading a little west of south. They were riding into the roughest part of the mountains, Longarm realized, an area where Sheriff Gray would have more trouble trailing them. There was a chance the women might be able to avoid the posse, at least for a while.

They stopped to rest the horses when the sun was a little past its zenith. Longarm and Dewey had their own canteens and food in their saddlebags, and Myra said that was good. "I don't want to have to feed you."

"You'd better let us go," Dewey warned her. "Holding us prisoner will just make things worse for you when Sheriff Gray catches up to you."

Longarm didn't say anything about Gray's plan to bring any of the fugitives he caught back to Fort Stockton as corpses. Dewey wouldn't have believed it, and it wouldn't have really changed anything. Instead he asked casually, "What are you planning to do, make a run for Mexico?"

Bridget started to nod. "We thought that's what we would do—"

"No," Myra interrupted. "Not yet."

The other four women looked at her, seemingly surprised by her answer. Abigail said, "I know we haven't talked about it, but I figured we would head for the border, too."

"If I'm going to spend the rest of my life on the run, I don't want to do it poor," said Myra. That was all she would say about what she had in mind, though.

Bridget went over to Dewey and pointed to the scrape on his face. "That looks like it hurts."

108

He winced. "It's pretty painful, all right. And I hurt from that spill I took. I hope nothing's all busted up inside."

"What's your name?"

"Dewey Carmichael. What's yours?"

"Bridget Powell."

"Bridget . . . that's a pretty name."

She blushed. A few yards away, Myra grimaced angrily and turned her back toward the two of them. Longarm took note of that. Myra peered back in the direction they had come from, no doubt searching for any telltale sign of dust in the sky. Longarm didn't see any, and he wondered if Sheriff Gray was really coming after them, as Longarm had predicted he would do.

Longarm put the cap back on his canteen, then, aware that the other women were keeping a suspicious eye on him, strolled over to Myra. She glanced at him once, then ignored him.

"What you said a few minutes ago about being poor," he said. "Seems to me that if the five of you just robbed a bank, money would be the least of your worries right about now."

"We didn't rob that bank," said Myra, still not looking at Longarm. "Some son of a bitch beat us to it. He killed one of the men inside before we left, and he must've shot the other two as we were running out of there. I heard a couple of shots behind us. But we didn't get any money. There was nothing there but petty cash."

"Who's this other fella you say was there?"

Myra shrugged as she finally looked at Longarm again. "His name was Durrell. We never saw him before."

Longarm scraped a thumbnail along the line of his jaw for a moment as he thought that over, then said, "You mind if I light up a cheroot?"

"Not if you give me one, too."

He had several of the little cigars in his shirt pocket. He took out a couple of them and handed one to Myra. "They got a mite bent up when I kept jumping off my horse," he said.

"They'll still smoke." Before Longarm could fish out a

109

lucifer, Myra had a match of her own burning. She lit both cheroots and inhaled deeply on her own.

"You know, I don't reckon I've met too many gals just like you."

Her lips curved slightly in a wry smile. "That's the damned truth."

"You really didn't rob that bank, did you?"

"Why would I lie to you about that, Marshal? We're already wanted by all the lawmen in West Texas. It doesn't matter whether or not we held up a bank." She puffed on the cheroot and blew smoke in the air. "I just don't like being blamed for killings I didn't do."

"Well, I'll remember what you've told me when it comes time for your trial."

Myra looked at him again, her eyes flat and cold. "Won't never be no trial. We'll either make it . . . or they won't take us alive."

Sheriff Ed Gray was still gripped by a killing rage. Having to turn tail and run was bad enough. Being forced to flee for his life by a bunch of women was even worse.

"All right, get on back to Fort Stockton," he told the four wounded men when the posse finally stopped its panicked retreat. "You're no use to me now."

One of the men, the one who was shot in the belly, would never make it to Fort Stockton, Gray knew. He would die a long the way. The others weren't hurt too bad; one had a bullet-shattered arm while the other two had just lost chunks of meat to the bushwhackers' slugs.

Hartley was dead, and Karnes and Long had galloped off around that ridge and not come back, so they were probably dead too, mused Gray as his men rested their horses and bound up a few minor bullet burns. Losing the four men he was sending back to town left him with just under a dozen. Still enough to get the job done, he told himself. All he had to do was catch up to those bitches. They wouldn't take him by surprise a second time.

The sheriff was certain the bushwhackers had been the

women who escaped from the prison wagon. He had caught a glimpse or two of broad-brimmed Stetsons up there on top of the ridge while the posse was trying futilely to fight back, so he knew Apaches weren't responsible for the ambush. That left just the fugitives he was seeking, unless there was some other bunch down here in the middle of nowhere that didn't like lawmen. A possibility, he conceded, but a remote one.

"Rider comin', Sheriff," one of the remaining members of the posse said, breaking into Gray's sullen reverie.

Gray looked up, saw a single man on horseback riding in from the west. He drew his gun, not knowing who this stranger could be, and the rest of the posse followed suit. As the rider drew closer, Gray saw that he had thick, sandy hair curling around his shoulders and several days' worth of beard stubble on his face. A gun was holstered on his hip, and a rifle rode in a saddle boot, the stock of it sticking up under the man's left thigh. He reined in and looked around at the posse with a smile.

"Howdy, boys," he said. "You won't need those guns. We're on the same side."

"What side's that?" asked Gray, not holstering his revolver just yet.

"Why, the side of law and order, of course. I see your badge there on your vest, Sheriff. Don't have a star of my own, but I'm a legally empowered officer of the law myself." The stranger thumbed back his hat and introduced himself. "Pete Durrell, constable up at Van Horn. You wouldn't by any chance be looking for a bunch of female owlhoots, would you?"

Gray frowned in surprise. "How do you know about them?"

"They robbed the bank in Van Horn a couple of days ago, killed the bank president, the teller, and a customer who was in there. I led a posse after them, but they gave us the slip. I sent the other boys on back to town, but I figured I'd stay on the trail a while myself." Durrell crossed his hands on the saddlehorn and leaned forward a little in the saddle to ease sore muscles. "I surely do hate to let a bunch of lawbreakers

111

get away. I heard some shooting over this way a while ago, thought I'd better check it out.''

Gray nodded, coming to an abrupt decision. Durrell looked like he could handle himself in a fight, and one more man might come in handy somewhere down the trail. The sheriff slid his Colt back into its holster and said, ''Light and set, Durrell. I reckon we're after the same bunch, all right, and you're welcome to ride with us.''

Durrell swung down from his horse. ''Much obliged, Sheriff. Us lawmen got to stick together.''

Myra turned west before she had led the group very far into the mountains. Longarm wondered what she was up to. She had already said they weren't making a run for the Rio Grande. She seemed to have some definite plan in mind, but if that was the case she wasn't sharing it with any of the others.

They stopped for the night on a pine-dotted bench at the base of a peak with a jagged, sawtooth summit. It was a cold camp, of course, another in a long string of them for Longarm. He was beginning to wonder if he would ever have hot food and coffee again as he sat on a fallen log and gnawed on a stale biscuit and a strip of jerky. He closed his eyes and thought about dinner in his favorite restaurant in Denver, steaks fried just right, mounds of potatoes, rolls still warm from the oven so that steam rose from them when they were pulled apart . . .

A loud rumble came from his stomach, and Longarm sighed. He supposed such thoughts maybe weren't a good idea after all.

Dewey was talking to that Bridget gal again, Longarm noticed. Their voices were pitched quiet, so he couldn't overhear what they were saying. But he could see the way Myra stood stiffly on the other side of the camp, looking toward the two of them. If he had been able to make out her features in the shadows, Longarm would be willing to bet that she didn't look happy. Apparently, his offhand comment earlier in the day about Myra not liking men in general had some truth to

112

it. Which also, apparently, meant that she had a fondness for women instead, and Bridget in particular.

"Would you like another biscuit?"

The question took him by surprise. He glanced up to see one of the women standing there, and he thought he recognized her voice as belonging to the blonde called Abigail. She was holding her hand out to him.

He took the biscuit from her. "Sure you don't need it?"

"We have plenty. We may not have any money, but we're not low on supplies yet." Abigail surprised him again by moving closer and sitting down on the log beside him. Not too close, Longarm noted, but within arm's reach if that's what he had in mind.

He didn't know what he had in mind right now. He could lunge at Abigail and probably get his hand on her gun, but that would lead to shooting because Myra would sure as hell try to kill him. He had come along with Gray so that the sheriff wouldn't kill these women, and Longarm still didn't want any of their deaths on his head.

He stayed where he was, munching on the biscuit Abigail had given him.

She took her hat off and sighed. "What would happen," she asked quietly, "if we turned ourselves in?"

Longarm thought about the question for a moment before saying, "Well, I reckon that would depend on how you came to escape from that prison wagon and what all you've done since then."

"What happened to the driver and the guard wasn't our fault. I swear we didn't have anything to do with it."

"Why don't you tell me about it?" suggested Longarm.

For the next few minutes she explained about the flooded creek, the washed-out bridge, and the driver's determination to cross the stream at Springer's Ford. What she was saying agreed almost perfectly with the theory Gray had laid out a few days earlier. She told Longarm about how the wagon had been swept away and how the driver and the guard had been killed in the accident.

"What about the other woman who was with you?" asked Longarm.

"She . . . drowned."

Longarm didn't believe her for a second, but he went along with the fiction. "What about her body? We didn't see it along the creek."

"We took it with us and buried her away from the creek."

That was remotely possible, Longarm supposed, although it didn't agree with the story the tracks had told. He let that go for now and said, "What then?"

"We stole some horses and clothes and guns from a ranch. The rancher didn't catch us."

That didn't sound too likely, either, but again Longarm let it pass. "Go on."

"We went to Van Horn to rob the bank there. You know about that."

"But you didn't actually rob it."

"What Myra told you was the truth."

"So you haven't actually killed anybody except the gent whose untimely demise got you sent off to prison."

"And he had it coming," said Abigail, her voice even lower and more intent now. "I was willing to serve my sentence for that. It . . . seemed a small price to pay." She took a deep breath. "But I don't want to be an . . . an outlaw. Always on the run, always worrying about being caught. Neither does Deborah."

"Your sister?"

"Yes."

Longarm was about to say something else when a cold ring of metal was pressed against the back of his neck. He recognized it immediately as the barrel of a gun.

"Why don't you just wait until he's gone to sleep and then crawl into his bedroll with him?" Myra said bitterly.

Longarm had been paying such close attention to Abigail that he hadn't noticed Myra moving over behind the log where they were sitting. Now Abigail sprang up and said, "I wasn't doing anything, Myra. Marshal Long and I were just talking—"

"I heard you," Myra said with a sneer in her voice. "Talking about turning yourself in, that's what you were doing. Giving up, after all I've done for you." Her voice rose in anger. "Giving up, just when I'm planning to make us all rich!"

She had the attention of everyone in the camp now. Timothea said, "Rich? How are you going to make us rich?"

"There's a whole strongbox full of cash headed for Van Horn three days from now, and it's going to be ours, by God!"

A strongbox full of cash? Now that was mighty interesting, thought Longarm.

He would have probably thought about it some more, if Myra hadn't chosen that moment to haul off and clout him on the head with the barrel of her pistol. Longarm pitched forward off the log into darkness even thicker than that which cloaked the mountains.

Chapter 14

Longarm had been knocked out enough times in his career as a lawman to know that the pain in his head when he woke up was a good thing. It told him right away that he was still alive.

He moved his head a little and winced as the pounding inside his temples intensified. Then cool fingertips moved soothingly across his forehead, and a voice murmured, "Take it easy, Marshal. Don't try to move."

Other than his head, there wasn't much about him that he *could* move, Longarm discovered a moment later. His wrists were bound together, and so were his feet. Somebody had hogtied him.

Myra. Had to be, thought Longarm. That gal had a plumb crazy streak in her, otherwise she wouldn't have walloped him like that for no good reason.

"You'll be all right," the voice said again, and this time Longarm recognized it as belonging to Abigail. He managed to open his eyes and saw her face close to his. Faint light from the stars penetrated the canopy of pine branches, and the illumination gave her blonde hair an inconstant glow, much like that of a will-o'-the-wisp. Her breath was warm against his face.

"Myra said I ought to crawl into your bedroll," whispered Abigail. "I'll bet she didn't think I'd actually do it."

Neither had Longarm, but at this elevation the nights were

cool and he was grateful for the warmth of her body pressed against his. He wasn't actually in a bedroll, but somebody had spread his blankets over him where he lay beside the fallen log. Abigail was under there with him.

"Where's everybody else?" asked Longarm, whispering since that was what Abigail had done.

"They're all asleep except for Deborah. She's standing guard."

"Over us, or the camp?"

"Both, I guess you could say." Abigail hesitated, then went on, "Marshal Long, you must think this is terribly forward of me."

"No such thing," he assured her. His headache was fading a little now. "I'm glad for the company."

"It's just that it's been a long time since I . . . since I've been around a man as handsome as you." She brushed a fingertip along the curving lines of his mustache. The caress tickled, but it sent a little shiver of desire through Longarm at the same time.

"After everything I went through, I thought I'd never want to be this close to a man again," Abigail continued. "But as soon as I saw you, Marshal Long, I found myself wanting you. Odd, isn't it?"

Under the circumstances, damned odd, thought Longarm, but he didn't say anything. Abigail seemed content to do the talking.

"A woman becomes accustomed to male contact, I suppose," she said. "And after so long a time . . ." Her hand slid down over his chest and stomach to his groin, where she cupped the hardening length of his shaft through his trousers. "Well, I . . . I just have to touch you, Marshal Long."

"Custis," he said. "My friends call me Custis."

"All right . . . Custis." She undid the buttons on his trousers and slipped her hand inside, closing her fingers around his pole. She quickly worked it free, so that it stood up hard and proud from his groin.

"Oh, my goodness," Abigail breathed. "It's so thick I can't get my fingers all the way around it." She gripped the shaft tightly around its base and moved her hand slowly up to the top. The milking motion made a drop of fluid ooze from the slit in the head. She rubbed her thumb over it and then around and around, spreading the moisture. Involuntarily, Longarm's hips bucked upward.

Abigail squeezed harder. Longarm ground his teeth together. This was sheer torture, having her do this to him while he was bound hand and foot and couldn't reciprocate. All he could do was lie there while she caressed him. She seemed to be satisfied with having a handful of hard male flesh, however. Her breath was coming faster now, and Longarm's eyes had adjusted sufficiently to the darkness for him to be able to see that her eyes were closed.

She rubbed and stroked and petted for a while, and Longarm thought he was going to go crazy. She was lying half on top of him now. Her mouth found his. Her lips were already parted, her tongue thrusting out to spear into his mouth. The kiss was long and hard and wet, and Longarm's shaft throbbed almost painfully in her grip.

Finally, Abigail took her lips away from his and said, "Lie as still as you can."

There wasn't much else Longarm could do, tied up as he was.

"My late husband used to force me to do this," she whispered. "I want to see what it's like when it's my idea."

With that, she slid down his body and took the crown of his manhood in her mouth. Longarm bit back a groan as she used the tip of her tongue to toy with the opening in the head. Then she opened her lips wider, took even more of the shaft into her mouth, and started sucking.

Longarm had already endured enough exquisite torment that he knew he couldn't hold off for long now. Sure enough, within moments he felt his climax boiling up. The thick white seed raced along the length of his shaft and burst out into her mouth, spurt after shuddering spurt. Abigail clamped her lips more tightly around the pole of flesh and swallowed what he gave her. Longarm's hips had risen off the ground again, and his whole body was curved and quivering like a bow as he emptied himself into the hot, wet cavern of her mouth.

Finally, Longarm was sated. His hips sagged back onto the ground. Abigail tucked his manhood back into his trousers and fastened the buttons, then moved over him again, lying on top of him with her head pillowed on his broad chest. Her own chest was heaving from whatever emotions were coursing through her, and with each deep breath her breasts were pressed against his belly. Her arms were around him, holding him tightly, and Longarm wished he could return the favor.

When she had recovered enough to be able to speak again, she lifted her head and said, "Deborah and I won't let Myra hurt you or the deputy. I don't know what we'll do yet, but be ready in case trouble comes."

"I'll be ready," Longarm promised her.

"I've got to go. . . ." She moved away from him, slipping out from under the blankets and standing up. Almost soundlessly, she vanished into the darkness.

Longarm could have almost thought he had dreamed the whole strange episode. Yet he knew it had actually happened; he had never had a dream that vivid—and exciting—in his life. Exhaustion crept over him, and he dozed off, wondering what the next day was going to bring.

It brought trouble, all right, but not the sort that Longarm expected.

He woke up to find Myra screaming at Bridget, "Don't lie to me, damn you! I know you were with him last night!"

"We were just talking, Myra!" Bridget defended herself. "I swear it!"

Longarm managed to sit up. He knew that Bridget hadn't been anywhere near *him*—but he wasn't the only man in camp, either. Dewey was tied up, too, and sitting with his back braced against a rock. From the shame-faced expression Dewey wore, Longarm knew the two women were arguing over the young deputy.

Myra and Bridget stood near Dewey, facing each other, Myra looking furious and Bridget shifting her feet uncomfortably. Abigail, Deborah, and Timothea were scattered around the camp, watching uncertainly.

"You swore you loved me," Myra said. "And I was damn fool enough to believe it."

"I do love you," insisted Bridget. "But Dewey seems like a nice young fella, and I just thought—"

"You just thought you'd have yourself a romp with him, maybe find out what you've been missing!" Myra's hands tightened on the Winchester in her grip as she swung it toward Dewey. He recoiled as best he could against the rock, eyes wide with horror, as he saw the barrel line up with his crotch. "Maybe I ought to just blow it off, so you won't be tempted no more!"

"Damn it, Myra, no!" Bridget yelled as she threw herself at the redhead. She tackled Myra around the waist, and the impact sent both women tumbling off their feet. Myra lost her hold on the rifle and it went sailing away.

Both of them were spitting and punching. and clawing as they landed on the ground and rolled over a couple of times. Myra was fighting harder, but Bridget weighed more and was stronger. They looked to be pretty evenly matched.

Abigail moved swiftly, and what she was doing interested Longarm a hell of a lot more than the cat fight between Myra and Bridget. The blonde stepped over behind him and bent down, and he felt something tug at the ropes around his wrists. "Don't move," hissed Abigail. "I'll cut you loose."

A couple of seconds later Longarm felt the bonds fall away. He moved his hands in front of him, easing the ache in his shoulders, and began flexing his fingers to get the blood flowing in them again. Meanwhile, Abigail hurried to his feet and slashed at the ropes there with a small knife. "I stole it from Myra," she said as she glanced up at Longarm.

He didn't care where she had gotten the knife, only that its blade was slicing through the bonds holding his feet together. As the ropes parted, he kicked loose from them and tried to stand up. His muscles betrayed him momentarily and made him stumble, but he caught himself with one hand against the trunk of a tree. As he looked up his eyes met those of Timothea, who was watching what was happening with an expression of disbelief. Clearly, she was torn about what to do next.

But then she decided, and a scream of alarm came from her mouth. "Myra!" she shrieked. "The marshal's loose!"

By this time, Bridget had managed to get on top of Myra, pinning her to the ground with her greater weight. Bridget was holding Myra's shoulders and trying to talk sense into her, but Timothea's shout made both of them turn their heads toward Longarm. Bridget was so surprised to see the lawman was loose that Myra was able to shove her to the side. Myra rolled over and scrambled up on her knees, reaching for the Colt at her hip as she did so.

Longarm didn't want to kill anybody. He shoved Abigail toward the horses and barked, "You and your sister get out of here!"

Abigail hesitated, then grabbed Deborah's hand and tugged on her. "Come on!" she said urgently. Wide-eyed with confusion and uncertainty, Deborah went, following the lead of her older sister as she had for most of her life.

Timothea brought up her rifle and fired, the blast loud in the early morning air. Longarm didn't know where the bullet went, but he was reasonably sure it hadn't come anywhere near him. A couple of strides brought him to Dewey's side, and without ever stopping he bent and scooped up the deputy, flinging him over his shoulder. Longarm staggered a little under Dewey's weight, but he managed to keep running. Another gun went off behind them, from the sound of it, Myra's Colt. Dewey yelped.

Abigail and Deborah had managed to get to a couple of the horses and were mounted on them. Abigail called to Longarm, "Over here! Put him in front of me!"

Handling Dewey like a sack of grain, Longarm slung the deputy over the back of the horse in front of Abigail. Dewey grunted in pain. Abigail grabbed hold of his belt with one hand to steady him and used the other hand to haul on the reins of the horse. The animal wheeled around and leaped into a gallop.

Longarm spun toward the horse Deborah was riding. In the past, he had seen trick riders jump on a horse from behind, but as far as Longarm was concerned that was a damned fool stunt and a good way for a fella to mash his balls. Instead, he lunged for the stirrup that was dangling free on the left side of the saddle, Deborah having had the foresight to slip her boot out of it. Longarm got his foot in it and grabbed the saddlehorn just as another shot rang out. The bullet smacked across the rump of the horse and made it leap forward with a shrill whinny of pain and outrage. Longarm hung on for dear life as his other foot was jerked off the ground.

He hoped like blazes that the cinch was good and tight.

Longarm's dangling right foot bounced off the ground a couple of times, then he was able to swing that leg up and over the horse's back. He was riding behind Deborah, one foot in the stirrup, an arm around her waist. Up ahead, the horse carrying Abigail and Dewey was racing across the ground. Longarm hoped Abigail had a firm hold on the deputy, otherwise he was liable to be jolted right off of there. Behind them, Myra, Bridget, and Timothea were still shooting. Slugs kicked up dust to both the right and the left of the fleeing horses, but none of them found their real targets. Longarm called out to Abigail, and when she glanced back he waved her toward another stand of pine.

They dashed into the trees. Abigail and Deborah reined in. Longarm slid to the ground, hardly able to believe that the entire escape had taken less than a couple of minutes. The action had been so fast and furious that it had seemed longer than that, a phenomenon with which Longarm was all too familiar.

"Give me your gun," Longarm snapped at Deborah.

She hesitated a second until Abigail said, "Do it." Then Deborah pulled the pistol from its holster and extended it butt-first to Longarm. He took the Colt and ran to the edge of the trees, half-crouching as he looked back across the bench toward the camp.

He halfway expected to see the other three women coming after them, guns blazing, but instead he heard the rapid patter

123

of hoofbeats and saw flickers of movement through the trees. They were riding off, he realized, making good their own escape while they had the chance. Myra had to be unhappy about losing her hostages and a couple of members of her group, but she was the type to move on and make the best of a situation, whatever it was. Longarm had realized that about her after hearing the tale of how she had led the escape from the prison wagon.

Deborah helped Dewey down, and Abigail used the knife to cut him loose. He was breathing hard and his face was pale and pinched with pain. Abigail asked, "Are you hit?"

Dewey shook his head and grimaced. "Nope. I landed on the saddlehorn when Marshal Long threw me on that horse. Like to punched a hole in my guts."

"You'll get over it," Longarm said as he rejoined the others. "We're all damned lucky we don't have any fresh bullet holes in our hides."

"What about Myra and Bridget and Timothea?" asked Abigail.

Longarm inclined his head toward the other side of the bench. "They lit a shuck out of there. I reckon Myra figured out that in a gunfight, we might all wind up dead. She didn't want that."

"She wants that money," said Deborah. "That's all she's interested in, that and being a famous outlaw."

"I wouldn't mind hearing more about that strongbox she mentioned," said Longarm, "but not just yet. Let's put a little more distance between us and them." He holstered Deborah's Colt in his empty cross-draw rig rather than giving it back to her. That pistol, and the one Abigail was carrying, were their only guns. The rifles had been left back in camp, and Longarm was sure Myra would have gathered them up before she and the other two women lit out.

They continued to ride double, only this time Longarm and Abigail shared a mount while Deborah and Dewey took the other horse. Longarm found a game trail that led generally northeast and followed it. That would take them toward the area where he had last seen Sheriff Gray and the rest of the posse.

As they rode, Abigail told Longarm more about the strongbox Durrell had mentioned back in Van Horn. "I don't really know much," she said. "The cash was supposed to be for the bank there, and it was due in on the train a few days ago. But it was delayed for some reason, and it wasn't supposed to come in until the next train arrived."

"Reserve banks like the one in El Paso send out shipments of cash like that to new banks," Longarm told her, "but they keep it a secret when they do. This fella Durrell must've found out about it somehow. He's liable to go after that train and try to get his hands on the loot that way."

Abigail nodded. "That's what Myra had in mind, I'm sure." She laughed humorlessly. "She wasn't able to turn us into successful bank robbers, so I guess she was going to try to make us train robbers next."

Longarm chuckled. "Just like the James boys. That gal's got one messed-up mind, I'm thinking."

"There were times when she seemed to genuinely care about all of us," mused Abigail. "Even though she didn't really like any of us except Bridget." She shrugged. "Other times I got the feeling that Myra was just using us to get what *she* wanted."

"I reckon that's true of just about everybody now and then," said Longarm.

Abigail was riding in front of him, so she had to turn her head in order to look back at him. "And what are *you* going to do now, Custis?"

Longarm had already given that question considerable thought. He said, "I'm afraid you're not going to like the answer . . . and neither do I."

Chapter 15

As unlikely to succeed as any attempt by the three women to
rob the train might be, Longarm knew he couldn't just ignore
what Myra was planning to do. He had a little time before the
train carrying the strongbox of cash was due to arrive in Van
Horn, enough time so that he could find Sheriff Gray and the
posse, turn Abigail and Deborah over to them, and then try to
stop whatever crazy scheme Myra might come up with for
robbing the train.

"I don't mind going to prison," Deborah said when they
stopped to rest the horses at midday. "I'd rather do that than
be an outlaw the rest of my life."

"I agree," said Abigail. "Like I told you, Custis, that's the
price we have to pay for what we did."

Longarm held up a hand. "No need to go into that. This
ain't a courtroom. And if I wasn't sworn to uphold the law, I
might have to give some serious thought to letting you ladies
go."

"You couldn't do that," Abigail said without hesitation.
"Not and live with yourself."

"But I intend to see that you get a fair shake. What happened with that prison wagon wasn't your fault, and neither
was that botched bank robbery. And according to what Myra
said, neither one of you actually hit anybody when you were
shooting at that posse."

The sisters exchanged a look, and Abigail said, "I was aiming over their heads, and I think Deborah was, too."

"I was," Deborah said. "I didn't want to hurt anybody."

Dewey looked skeptical. "You actually believe what these women are telling you, Marshal?" he asked.

Longarm nodded and said, "I do. And if you've got any sense, you will, too. After all, they risked their lives to get you away from the others before we each wound up with a bullet through the head."

"Aw, Bridget wouldn't have hurt us," protested Dewey. "Her and me got along pretty good."

"All the more reason Custis is right," said Abigail. "That would have been enough to make Myra kill you right there."

Dewey frowned. "Why in the world would she want to go and do that, just because Bridget was acting friendly toward me?"

Longarm clapped a hand on the deputy's shoulder. "Somebody'll have to explain that to you later on, old son. Right now, we got to get moving again."

Myra wanted to shoot something. Specifically, Marshal Custis Long, damn him. But the mood she was in, almost anything would do, which was why Bridget and Timothea rode behind her in silence, from time to time exchanging a nervous glance.

Finally, Myra's rage subsided a little, and she looked back at Timothea and said, "I'm surprised you didn't go with them."

"I thought about it," Timothea said honestly. "But then I thought about that strongbox full of cash. I'd rather have a chance at that than the certainty of going to prison."

Myra summoned up a chuckle. "You may be a fancy pants, Thea, but you got plenty of larceny in your soul."

"I never claimed otherwise."

Seeing that Myra was in a better frame of mind, Bridget ventured, "I really didn't do anything with Dewey except talk to him, Myra. I swear it."

Myra shrugged. "I reckon I believe you. Well, he's gone now, and so is Long. And good riddance to those other two, running out on us like they did. They're no better'n that whore Ginny.''

"Abigail and Deborah weren't so bad," said Timothea. "They were nice to me."

"And not worth a wet fart in a gunfight. I don't think either of them hit a damned thing when we threw down on that posse." Myra spat off to the side. "No, we're better off without 'em. They'd have just gotten in the way when we go to rob that train."

"How are we going to do that?" asked Timothea.

Myra shook her head. "Don't know just yet. I'll have to get the lay of the land first. But I'll tell you this—that train will never get to Van Horn with that money on it."

Pete Durrell slipped a flask from his saddlebag and took a quick nip from it as Sheriff Gray called a halt. Durrell looked around him at the faces of the other members of the posse. They were bone-tired, weary from a couple of days of riding back and forth through the foothills looking for some sign of those women. For a plugged nickel, most of them would have turned around and gone home.

But Gray wasn't going to allow that. The sheriff was like a dog with a bone in his teeth. He wasn't going to give it up.

Durrell didn't intend to give up, either. He wanted those women dead. They were the only ones who had any idea he had killed the banker and the teller back in Van Horn. Durrell hadn't had any choice in the matter. Once it had become apparent that his plan had gone awry, he had to get rid of the witnesses. Otherwise his carefully prepared cover as the settlement's constable would have been ruined. And since those sweet ladies were right there so handy to take the blame for the killings . . .

The plan had come together quickly in Durrell's brain. He had made sure the posse he led from Van Horn didn't catch up to the women, because he couldn't very well kill them in cold blood in front of a dozen solid citizens, now could he? And after he'd sent the posse back to town and carried on by himself, his only goal had been to find the women, get the drop on them because they would take him for another owl-hoot, not a lawman, and then kill them before he went after the train carrying that strongbox.

Running into this other posse had been a mixed blessing. Durrell didn't need the witnesses to what he planned to do, but at the same time he sensed a kindred spirit in Sheriff Ed Gray. Gray was out for whatever would make him the biggest profit, and Durrell was just biding his time before he let the sheriff in on the secret of the cash shipment from El Paso. The two of them could take that train and split the loot. Durrell already had the spot in mind where he would stop the loco-motive, a long slope that would force the train to slow down considerably. He could ride up out of an arroyo that the tracks crossed on a trestle and be in the cab before the engineer and the fireman knew what was happening. All he would have to do then was force them to stop the train and help himself to the strongbox in the caboose. It might be easier, though, if he had somebody like Gray to back his play. The conductor might give trouble, and so might some of the passengers.

Those thoughts were spinning through Durrell's head as he took off his hat, poured some water in it, and let his horse drink. While he was doing that, someone called, "Riders comin' in, Sheriff!" Durrell looked up to see a pair of horses approaching the posse. Each of the animals appeared to be carrying double.

Suddenly, Durrell stiffened. He caught glimpses of fair-haired figures on both of the horses, riding behind the men who were handling the reins. Two of those women from the bank in Van Horn had been blondes, he recalled. Quickly, he dumped the rest of the water from his hat, clapped it on his head, and pulled the brim down. Moving casually so that he wouldn't draw any undue attention, he took hold of his horse's reins and drifted back toward the rear of the posse, where the newcomers wouldn't be able to get a good look at him.

Durrell's instincts had served him well. A couple of minutes later, the four people on horseback dismounted in front of Sheriff Gray, who had strode forward to meet them. Durrell recognized the women. They had been part of that bunch in the bank, all right.

Well, this was a complication he didn't need, he thought, but it didn't really matter. That money was going to be his, and he didn't care who had to die for him to get it.

Longarm swung down from the saddle and then helped Abigail dismount. A few feet away, Dewey gave Deborah a hand. And Sheriff Gray just stared at each of them in turn, as if he didn't know who to be more amazed at seeing. His face became more and more flushed.

Finally, he erupted. "Dewey?" he burst out. "What the hell are you doing here?" Before the deputy could answer, Gray turned toward Longarm. "And Long! I thought you were dead!"

"Not hardly," replied Longarm. "No thanks to you, Sheriff."

Gray's mouth tightened into a thin line. "I had to think about the other members of the posse," he said. "Those bushwhackers would've killed us all if we'd stayed there on that trail."

He might have a point about that, thought Longarm. Myra would have wiped out the posse if she could.

Gray nodded at the two women. "I reckon these are a couple of those escaped prisoners?"

"That's right," said Longarm. "They're turning themselves in. That ought to weigh on their side when it comes time for a judge to decide what to do with them."

Gray rubbed his beard-stubbled jaw and finally nodded. "Yeah, I suppose so." Longarm thought he looked faintly disappointed. Gray had planned on collecting the rewards on the corpses of the fugitives, and now he had two live women on his hands, women who he couldn't very well gun down in cold blood in front of the posse.

The sheriff looked over at Dewey and went on, "You still haven't told me what you're doing here. I left you back in Fort Stockton."

Dewey held on to the reins of his horse and shifted his feet nervously. "I came to warn you, Sheriff."

"Warn me? Warn me about what?"

"That the prisoners you went after were women. Another telegram came in from the sheriff in El Paso."

Gray snorted in contempt. "We figured out they were women," he said.

"But you didn't know they robbed a bank in Van Horn and killed a bunch of folks," Dewey said, eager to impress his boss.

"That's a long story," Longarm put in, "and I reckon it can wait until later. Right now, Sheriff, there are some other things I need from you, namely a rifle, a fresh horse, and some supplies."

"What the hell are you up to, Long?" Gray asked with a frown. "You planning on going after the rest of those women by yourself?"

"Nope. This is a federal matter." Which was true enough, thought Longarm. That shipment of cash from the reserve bank belonged to Uncle Sam, and as the old boy's only duly appointed representative here in West Texas at the moment, it was up to Longarm to keep it from getting stolen.

"Well, I reckon we can spare what you need," Gray said grudgingly. He jerked a thumb at Abigail and Deborah, who had so far remained quiet. "What do I do with these two?"

"I'd send Dewey and a couple of men back to Fort Stockton with them, if it was me," said Longarm. "They won't give you any more trouble."

"That's right, Sheriff," said Abigail, speaking up for the first time. "We're tired of running. We just want to go back and take what's coming to us."

"You'll do that, all right," Gray said. He looked at Dewey. "Think you can get them back to town without losing 'em?"

Dewey's back stiffened. "Yes, sir, I sure can."

With a grunt, Gray said, "All right, you're in charge, then. Get whatever supplies you need and start back this afternoon. But before you go . . ." Gray looked at Abigail and Deborah and asked harshly, "Where are the others?"

."One of them drowned in the creek," Abigail said, and Longarm thought the lie was coming easier to her now. "The last time we saw the others, they were back there in the foothills." She pointed to the south.

"Is that true, Long?"

"It's the gospel," Longarm told the sheriff. And it was true, as far as it went.

"Damn it, I wish you'd take us there so we could pick up the trail."

Longarm shook his head. "Like I said, I've got an errand to tend to for the federal government. But if you go on up this valley about ten miles, then cut through a pass over to the next one to the west and follow it to a bench at the base of that sawtoothed mountain you can see over yonder in the distance, you'll be able to pick up their trail."

Of course, Myra and the other two would be long gone before Gray and his men could get there, but Longarm didn't see fit to add that little bit of information. A day and a night and half of another day had passed since Myra, Bridget, and Timothea had taken off from that campsite, heading one way while Longarm and his companions had gone in another direction.

"All right," said Gray. "You're in charge of the prisoners, Dewey. Pick a couple of men to ride with you, and get started back to Fort Stockton."

"Yes, sir!"

Gray gave Longarm one of the spare rifles and let him pick out another horse. Longarm put more jerky and hardtack in his saddlebags once he had switched saddles. He was worn out, but he didn't have time to rest yet. It would take him the remainder of the day and some of the next to reach Van Horn, and he had no idea what time of day the train carrying the money was due to arrive. Myra would almost certainly try to stop it west of town, so Longarm would have to follow the tracks from Van Horn in hopes of meeting the train before Myra could make her move.

He mounted up and nodded to Gray. "Good luck," he said to the sheriff, not really meaning it. It would be perfectly all right with Longarm if Gray and the rest of the posse just wandered around in the Davis Mountains on a wild goose chase for the next couple of days.

"Good luck to you," Gray replied, and Longarm suspected the sheriff meant it just about as much as he had.

Longarm turned the horse, heeled it into motion, and rode off toward the northwest. He hoped Abigail and Deborah would be all right. If any fatal "accidents" befell them on the way back to Fort Stockton, Ed Gray would be one sorry son of a bitch.

Because in that case, Longarm would just have to find some excuse to kill him.

Durrell stayed in the background and made sure the two women didn't notice him as the deputy called Dewey rounded up a couple of men, fresh horses for everybody, and some supplies for the trip back to Fort Stockton. He waited until the group had left before approaching Sheriff Gray.

"Where've you been?" Gray asked him suspiciously. "Long said those women held up the bank in Van Horn, and ain't that where you're from? I figured you'd want to question them."

Durrell shook his head. "They were two of the bunch, all right, but they're already in custody. The other three aren't."

"So you're riding on with us to look for them?"

"Well, I don't know, Sheriff. . . . Reckon I could have a word with you in private?"

Gray frowned. "What in blazes for?"

Durrell lowered his voice a little more. "Might be a profit in it for both of us."

Profit was the magic word where Ed Gray was concerned, all right. The sheriff's eyes lit up, and he inclined his head toward a large rock on the side of the trail. He and Durrell moved around on the other side of it.

"Spit it out," barked Gray when he was confident the rest of the posse couldn't overhear whatever Durrell had to say.

"The reason those women hit the bank in Van Horn was because the banker was expecting a shipment of new cash from the reserve bank in El Paso. Only it didn't get there on time.''

Durrell quickly laid out the situation—leaving out his own part in the deaths of the three men in the bank—and concluded by saying, ''That strongbox is now supposed to be on the next train to Van Horn from El Paso. It'll come in tomorrow sometime.''

Gray rubbed his jaw and grimaced. ''Why are you telling me all this, Durrell?''

''Thought it might give you some ideas, Sheriff,'' Durrell said with a grin.

Gray stiffened. His eyes narrowed, and for a second Durrell worried that maybe he had figured the lawman all wrong. But then Gray asked, ''How much money do you think will be in that strongbox?''

''Don't know for sure. But there'll be at least twenty or thirty thousand dollars, I reckon.''

''That's a lot of money,'' mused Gray.

''Damn right. Split two ways, at least ten grand apiece.''

Slowly, a grin spread across Gray's craggy features. ''Two men could probably stop that train and take the strongbox, couldn't they?''

''That's what I figure. There'll be a couple of guards in the caboose with it, but no more than that because the reserve bank and the railroad like to keep it mighty quiet when they ship cash.'' At least, that was what Herman Keller, the bank president, had let slip to Durrell, back when he still thought the constable was an honest lawman.

''It'd go easier with a couple more men,'' suggested Gray. ''Their shares wouldn't have to be as big.''

Durrell considered for a moment, then shrugged. ''I suppose that would be all right. Where would we find them?''

''There are a couple of gents in the posse I'd trust to ride with us: that gambler, Holloway, and one of the cowboys who calls himself O'Neil. He thinks I don't know he's on the dodge from some stagecoach robberies up in Kansas, but I do.''

''Sounds like they'd be all right,'' Durrell said with a nod. ''So, what about it, Sheriff? Are you with me?''

Gray pondered a moment longer, then leaned over and spat on the ground. "Hell," he said with a grin, "I was getting pretty damned tired of Fort Stockton anyway. With ten grand in my pocket, I wouldn't ever have to go back there." A thought suddenly occurred to him. "Say, I'll bet Long knows something about this. That's probably why he rode off in such a hurry."

"Could be," said Durrell. "You have a problem with taking him on if he gets in our way?"

The smile on Gray's face turned wolfish. "Problem, hell," he said. "I'd be glad for a chance to blow a hole in the bastard."

Chapter 16

Longarm had a pretty good idea where Van Horn was, so he headed northwest from where he had left Sheriff Gray and the posse from Fort Stockton. The last time Longarm had been to West Texas on an assignment, he'd wound up a good ways north and east of here, in the sand hills near the settlement of Monahans. This country north of the Davis Mountains, while fairly rugged and arid, was nothing like that blazing hell.

He rode all day, made yet another cold camp that night, and started off again the next morning. Within a couple of hours, he came across a wagon road that led in what he thought was the right direction, so he began following it. By noon he reached a crossroads, and the weathered signpost planted there told him he was only fifteen miles from Van Horn. Longarm pushed on.

When he reached his destination, he saw that the settlement didn't amount to much yet. The first thing he saw was the elevated water tank alongside the Texas & Pacific tracks. There wasn't a full-fledged depot, just a covered shed with a T & P signboard on it. A single street, broad and dusty, paralleled the tracks for a couple of hundred yards on the north side of the railroad right-of-way. The buildings were a fifty-fifty mix of adobe and frame structures.

Longarm reined his mount to a halt in front of Van Horn's only hotel. A couple of old-timers sat in cane-bottom chairs on the building's front porch, playing dominos on a rickety table placed between them. One of them made a play and moved a wooden peg three holes in a punchboard beside him. The other old man frowned and said, "That's only ten points, not fifteen."

"The hell you say!" exclaimed the other oldster. "Count them spots again."

His opponent pointed to each of the dominos on the ends of the intersecting strands and moved his lips as he counted to himself. After a moment, he shrugged and played one of his dominos. "Well, then, I reckon this must be twenty. And I domino, too."

The other old man turned his sole remaining domino face up. "Double blank," he cackled. "You ain't gettin' no more from me!"

Longarm said, "Howdy, fellas." Unless he spoke up, there was no telling how long the old men would continue with their game before they acknowledged him.

Both men turned to stare at him. Longarm knew he must not look too impressive. His coat, vest, and hat were long gone, and his face hadn't seen a razor in several days. Trail dust coated his clothes. But he had pinned his badge to his shirt before riding into Van Horn, and that was what the two old men focused on.

"Lawman," said one of them.

"Big young fella, too."

Longarm asked, "Is there a badge-toter around here?"

"We got us a constable, in case a fight breaks out down at the saloon."

"Where can I find him?"

"He ain't here," said the other old man. "Rode out a few days back on the trail o' some gals who robbed the bank and shot up the place."

"Took a posse with him," added the first old-timer, "but they come back empty-handed. Said Durrell was goin' to keep lookin' for them women."

Longarm grimaced. He'd hoped to find a lawman here in Van Horn who could lend him a hand, or at least provide him with some information. Instead the local law was somewhere down south of here, wandering around looking for Myra and the others. Longarm wondered if the man would run into Sheriff Gray and the posse from Fort Stockton.

"I heard the banker was dead," said Longarm. "Who's in charge of the bank now?"

"Nobody," replied one of the old-timers. "Only teller was killed, too. Place is locked up tighter'n a drum now. Herman Keller, he's the one who owned the bank, had a brother back in Fort Worth. Heard tell he's comin' out as soon as he can to get things straightened out, but there ain't no tellin' when he'll get here."

Longarm scrubbed a hand over his face in weariness. He asked, "Does the Texas & Pacific have an agent in town?"

"Ezzard Pride, over to the hardware store, handles freight shipments for 'em. Reckon he's as close to a railroad agent as we got hereabouts."

Longarm nodded and turned his horse's head. "Much obliged." He left the old men to their game and rode toward the hardware store. Van Horn appeared to have only one of every sort of establishment, so he didn't have any trouble finding it.

Ezzard Pride was a short, fat man with bushy burnside whiskers that came down nearly to his pudgy chin. He was more impressed by the sight of Longarm's badge than the two old men had been. "What can I do for you, Marshal?" he asked as soon as Longarm had come into the store and introduced himself.

"I hear you handle freight for the T & P," said Longarm.

"Yes, sir, I can write you up if you've got something you need to ship. The trains always stop here to take on water, so we don't even have to flag 'em down."

"You've got a schedule, then?"

"Sure do." Pride reached below the counter and brought up a cardboard placard. "The trains run pretty near on time, too."

The storekeeper turned the placard so that Longarm could read it. The westbound train from El Paso was due to arrive

139

in Van Horn at 4:17 that afternoon. Longarm put a blunt fingertip on the listing and said, "I don't reckon this one was early today, was it?"

Pride shook his head. "No, sir. Far as I know it's on schedule, though."

"I didn't see any telegraph wires as I was coming in to town."

"Nope, they haven't gotten here yet. Supposed to build the line sometime in the next couple of years, they tell me."

That was a shame. If there had been a telegraph in Van Horn, Longarm could have wired all the stops along the train's route and had it stopped before it ever got here with that shipment of cash for the now closed bank.

"Expecting any special freight today?" he asked.

Pride looked genuinely puzzled. "Not that I know of."

That made sense, thought Longarm. Neither the banker here in town, nor the folks at the reserve bank, would have had any reason to tell Pride about the strongbox full of money. Longarm was glad to see that its impending arrival wasn't common knowledge.

"Have you got a good map of the area?"

"Army topographical map do you?"

Longarm grinned and nodded. "That'll do fine."

Pride hunted up the map and spread it out on the counter. Longarm's grin vanished as he saw that the map had been drawn from an 1867 survey. The Texas & Pacific tracks weren't marked on it. For that matter, neither was Van Horn, which hadn't even existed until a few months earlier, let alone in 1867.

Longarm rested his palms on the counter and leaned over the map. "Can you show me where we are and how the railroad runs west of here?" he asked.

"Sure." Pride rested a fingertip on the map. "Right here is Van Horn. The tracks run thisaway—" His finger moved, tracing a westward route.

"What's the next settlement to the west?"

"That'd be Sierra Blanca." Pride poked his finger at another spot on the map. "Right here between the Sierra Diablo to the north and Devil Ridge to the south."

"Surrounded by devils," muttered Longarm. Sometimes he felt the same way. His eyes narrowed as he studied the map, taking in all the physical features between the towns of Sierra Blanca and Van Horn. Somewhere in there, Myra would try to stop the train and steal that strongbox, he thought.

He stabbed a finger at a meandering line on the map. "Is this a dry wash?"

Pride squinted at the area where Longarm was pointing. "I believe so, 'cept when it comes a good rain. I imagine it was running for a while after that gullywasher they had up in New Mexico Territory a couple of weeks ago, but it's probably dry again by now."

Some of the runoff that had come roaring down that arroyo had probably wound up in Diablo Creek, mused Longarm. Another Diablo . . . General William Tecumseh Sherman, Longarm recalled, had been quoted as saying that if he owned both Hell and Texas, he would rent out Texas and live in Hell. Obviously, folks out here who went around naming places felt sort of the same way.

"Is there a trestle over it?"

"Yep, best I recall from my last trip to El Paso."

"And from the arroyo the tracks climb a long grade."

"It's uphill for the next couple of miles, I'd say. Not real steep, but steep enough and long enough to make the train slow down considerable."

Longarm nodded. The same thought had been going through his head. Thinking like an owlhoot, that was what he was doing. He'd been chasing outlaws, desperadoes, and highbinders for so long that he supposed such thought processes were second nature to him now.

"I'm obliged to you, Mr. Pride," he said as he straightened. He turned toward the door of the hardware store.

"Marshal?"

Longarm paused and looked back, and the storekeeper asked, "What's this all about? Is there going to be some sort of trouble?"

"I hope not," Longarm answered honestly. Thinking of Myra, Bridget, and Timothea, he went on, "I've got to meet somebody, and I reckon we'll have to just wait and see what happens then."

Myra reined in and rolled her shoulders to ease the ache in them. Beside her, Bridget and Timothea brought their mounts to a halt.

They had stopped atop a long, rocky ridge that ran east and west for several miles. In the distance to the north, a range of low, rounded mountains ran at an angle. In between was a broad valley, and in the valley was a town.

"That's Sierra Blanca," Myra said as she nodded toward the settlement. She glanced at the sky. The sun was just about at its zenith. "I hope to hell we're in time."

"In time for what?" asked Bridget.

Timothea added, "Don't you think it's time you let us in on your plan?"

"I suppose," said Myra, "but we don't have any time to waste. Come on, I'll tell you while we're riding."

They walked their horses down the slope, taking care that the animals didn't slip on the rock-littered surface.

"There's no telegraph line between Van Horn and Sierra Blanca," Myra said, "so there's a good chance nobody over here knows anything about that bank robbery we tried to pull. I'll bet they don't know anything about that shipment of cash, either. The railroad and the reserve bank will be keeping that a secret."

"How did that fella Durrell know?" asked Bridget.

Myra shook her head. "I've been puzzling over that, but I don't have any answer. That banker knew him; I reckon Durrell must've hung around Van Horn long enough that everybody thought he was a respectable citizen before he made his try for the money. Anyway, I'm betting that we can ride into Sierra Blanca and get on that train as passengers."

"Without tickets?" That dubious comment came from Timothea.

Myra shrugged and said, "I haven't worked out that part

of it just yet. But I reckon we'll figure out a way. It's got to be easier stopping the train from inside than outside."

"How will we get away once we've got the money?" asked Bridget.

Myra's teeth ground together. Bridget and Timothea kept coming up with arguments. Unfortunately, the questions they asked were good ones. Myra was beginning to realize that there was more to being an outlaw than big ambitions and a willingness to shoot people if they got in your way.

"We need two people on the train," said Timothea, "and one outside to bring the horses. That way after we stop the train, we can get away."

Myra nodded. "Makes sense. Bridget, you're in charge of the horses. Thea and I will be on the train."

"Why can't I ride on the train?" Bridget protested, half-pouting.

"Because you're a good rider, and you can follow the train and lead the extra horses. Thea couldn't do that. And I need to be on the train in case we have to shoot anybody."

Timothea paled a little at that.

"All right," Bridget agreed grudgingly. "But you still haven't said how the two of you are going to get on the train without tickets."

"Oh, we'll have tickets," said Timothea.

Myra frowned. "How do you figure that?"

"We still have those dresses of Reuben's mother in our saddlebags. We need to get them out, shake some of the wrinkles out of them, and change into them before we get to Sierra Blanca." Timothea smiled confidently. "After that, just leave the rest to me."

Durrell, Gray, Holloway, and O'Neil circled wide around Van Horn, making sure to avoid the town. Durrell didn't want to run into anyone who would recognize him and wonder what he was doing there when he was supposed to be down south around the Davis Mountains, chasing those lady outlaws.

The four men had ridden hard after leaving the rest of the posse. Some of the other men from Fort Stockton had seemed a little skeptical of Gray's idea that the posse should split up, but he *was* the sheriff, and after all, two groups could cover twice as much ground as one. And the number of fugitives they were after had dwindled now to three—half of the original bunch. Those three were women, to boot. The other possemen didn't want to admit that they might have trouble handling three women.

So Gray, Durrell, Holloway, and O'Neil had headed west through the mountains while the other five men had gone east. As soon as they were well out of sight, Gray and the others had turned their horses and ridden northwest at a gallop.

That had been the day before. Now, after a lot of hard riding, they skirted Van Horn to the west and made their way to the tracks of the Texas & Pacific. It was nearly the middle of the afternoon when they reached the railroad.

"The place I have in mind is about ten miles farther on," explained Durrell. "It's a dry wash with a trestle over it. As soon as the train crosses the trestle, it starts up a grade and has to slow down."

"So we'll be hiding in the arroyo and we'll catch up to the train before it reaches the top of the grade," speculated Gray.

Durrell nodded. "That's the plan. Since we've got four men now, I reckon three of us will take the caboose. That way we'll outnumber the guards."

"Not counting the conductor," Gray pointed out.

"If he's in there. He might be somewhere else on the train. Anyway, the fourth man will ride on up to the engine and get into the cab. Kill the engineer and the fireman if you have to, just get the train stopped whatever it takes."

"Who's handling that job?" asked O'Neil, a stocky, sandy-haired puncher.

"I thought it might be a good job for you," replied Durrell. "The sheriff, Holloway, and I will handle the men in the caboose."

Both Gray and Holloway, the dark, lean-faced gambler, nodded in agreement. None of them would hesitate to shoot to kill. Holloway and O'Neil had been told that the strongbox they were after would contain cash, but not how much. Each

144

had agreed to take part in the robbery for a share of one thousand dollars apiece. They knew that Gray and Durrell stood to collect considerably more than that, but neither of the men particularly cared. A thousand each was still good money for a day's ride and a little gun work.

The afternoon wore on as they followed the railroad tracks. After a while, Gray asked worriedly, "How much farther is it to that dry wash you talked about, Durrell?"

"It's less than a mile to the top of the grade," Durrell answered. "From there it's about two miles down to the trestle. You'll see it soon enough."

"When's that train due again?"

"It's supposed to arrive in Van Horn at four-seventeen." Durrell fished a turnip watch out of his pocket and flipped it open.

"It's a little after three. We'll make it in plenty of time. That train's sometimes late, but it's never early."

"What's that, then?" Holloway asked dryly.

"What?" snapped Gray.

"Listen," advised the gambler.

They all heard it then, and their eyes widened with surprise. "Shit!" Durrell exploded.

Somewhere far in the distance to the west, a train was blowing its whistle. The shrill sound came to them faintly in the dry, high desert air.

Chapter 17

A couple of hours earlier, two women entered the post office at Sierra Blanca. As in Van Horn, there was no full-fledged railroad depot in the recently-established town, but the postmaster in Sierra Blanca served as the freight agent for the T & P. The man—a spare, middle-aged gent in shirt sleeves, vest, string tie, and a black visor—stood behind the post office wicket and looked curiously at the two women. He had never seen them before.

They were both damned pretty, at least to the eyes of a musty old bachelor like him. They wore homesteader dresses, but the one in the lead, the one with thick, curly brown hair, looked as if she was accustomed to something finer. She swept across the dusty planks of the post office floor as if they were the shining parquet of a southern plantation ballroom.

She gave him a brilliant smile and asked, "Are you Mr. Goodwin?"

"Yes, ma'am. Edgar Goodwin, United States Postmaster. What can I do for you?"

"I'm told that you can write tickets for my sister and I to take the train?"

Goodwin nodded. "Yes, ma'am." They didn't look much like sisters, he thought. The other one had bright red hair and pale skin that had been sunburned too often. But who was he to judge such things?

"Very good." The woman laid a hand with long, slender fingers on the counter. "We need two tickets to Fort Worth."

Goodwin rummaged under the counter and found his ticket book for the Texas & Pacific. It wasn't used very often, and he had to blow a thin layer of dust off it. He picked up a pen, dipped it in the inkwell on the counter, and started filling in the destination on the first ticket.

"You're in luck," he said as he wrote. "The eastbound's due today. Ought to be here in less than an hour, in fact. So you won't have to wait very long, ma'am."

She beamed across the counter at him and then turned to her sister. "You see, Euphegenia, I told you the train was due today. Good fortune is with us. I'm sure we—" The smile fell away from her face, and her voice broke slightly. "I'm sure we'll be at Father's bedside in time."

Goodwin frowned a little. "You ladies are going to see your pa?"

"Yes." The woman struggled to put a small, brave smile back on her face. "For the last time, I fear. Our poor father is . . . is dying."

The redhead lifted her hands and put them over her face, as if to conceal a look of grief.

"That's terrible," said Goodwin.

"Yes, it is. Euphegenia and I were staying at the Penders ranch, west of here, when we received word of our father's illness. We're distant relatives of Mrs. Penders, you know."

"No, ma'am," Goodwin said with a shake of his head. "I didn't know Emily Penders had any kin." His frown deepened. "Don't recall seeing any letters come through mailed to the Penders spread in the past day or so, either. And I'd know."

"Of course you would, you dear man. But you see, the situation is so grave that our brother in Dallas sent word of our father's illness by means of the telegraph to Pecos, and a rider from there brought the dreadful news directly to the ranch in order to save time."

"Your brother had somebody ride all the way from Pecos?"

"In circumstances such as these, money is no object," the young woman said gravely.

Goodwin scratched his head. "No, I reckon not." He went back to filling out the tickets. "Names?"

"Miss Amelia Peabody and Miss Euphegenia Peabody."

Goodwin scrawled the names in the appropriate blanks on the tickets, then looked up as something occurred to him. "I thought you said your father was in Fort Worth."

"Yes?" Miss Amelia Peabody allowed a touch of impatience to creep into her cultured voice.

"But you just said your brother wired from Dallas."

"Well, of course he did," she said. "Jasper's business is in Dallas. It's becoming quite the financial center, you know. But our father lives in Fort Worth."

"Oh." Goodwin nodded. "I reckon that makes sense." He scribbled a little more on the tickets, then said, "That'll be thirty-two dollars and forty-seven cents."

"Certainly." Miss Amelia turned to her sister. "Euphegenia?"

"What?" asked the redhead.

"You're carrying our funds. Please pay Mr. Goodwin."

Miss Euphegenia shook her head. "You brought the money," she said. "I saw you put your purse in the wagon when we left the ranch."

"Why, that's nonsense! I *know* you had our funds."

"I tell you, I don't," insisted the redhead. "You must have left your purse in the wagon when it went back to the ranch."

Miss Amelia's mouth opened into an O of surprise and dismay. She pressed her fingers to her cheeks. "Merciful heavens, I think you're right!" she exclaimed.

Goodwin tapped a blunt finger on the tickets. "I need thirty-two dollars and forty-seven cents, ladies."

Miss Amelia turned to look at him, her eyes wide and brimming with tears. "This . . . this is terrible!" she said. "Mr. Goodwin, we are forced to throw ourselves on your mercy! We simply must get to Fort Worth as soon as possible." As if to punctuate her words, a train whistle sounded in the distance. Miss Amelia let out a moan.

149

For a second, Goodwin had thought that the women were up to some sort of trick. But Miss Amelia's distress seemed genuine, and Miss Euphegenia looked pretty upset, too. Goodwin decided they had made an honest mistake. But still, rules were rules.

"I'd like to help you, ladies, but I can't give you these tickets unless you can come up with thirty-two dollars—"

"And forty-seven cents, we know," said Miss Euphegenia.

"You know Mr. and Mrs. Penders," said Miss Amelia.

"I'm sure they would be glad to pay you the next time they're in town. Or I could send you a bank draft as soon as we reach Fort Worth. I . . . I shall do it even before we go to the hospital to see Father."

"If he's still alive and kicking when we get there," added Miss Euphegenia.

Her sister shot a look of reprimand at her, probably for sounding a little callous. Obviously, Miss Euphegenia wasn't as close to her father as her sister was.

Miss Amelia turned those big, wet eyes back toward Goodwin. "Please, Mr. Goodwin." The rumble of the approaching locomotive grew louder. "I . . . I'm sure that as an official of the Texas & Pacific Railroad, you have some leeway in your procedures."

"Well . . ." Goodwin grimaced and rubbed his jaw. "I suppose I could bend the rules a mite this once. . . ."

Miss Amelia's face lit up. "Oh! Would you? Could you?"

"But only if you send me that bank draft as soon as you can," Goodwin said sternly. He grimaced again and added in a gentler tone, "After you've seen your pa, that is."

"I simply cannot thank you enough, Mr. Goodwin." Miss Amelia's hand shot out and snatched up the tickets from the counter. "You are a wonderful man!" Then she turned and practically ran for the door of the post office. "Come along, Euphegenia!" she flung over her shoulder. "We must get our bags. We don't want the train to leave without us!"

Myra caught up to Timothea just outside the post office. " 'Euphegenia'?" she said. "You call yourself Amelia, and you stick me with a moniker like that?"

Timothea sniffed and clutched the train tickets more tightly in her hand. "He believed me, didn't he? And you didn't help matters with that 'alive and kicking' comment of yours."

"Hell, he wasn't any different from any other man," Myra said with a snort of disgust. "A pretty gal bats her eyelashes at one of 'em and acts like she's about to cry, and he'll cut off his own balls and hand 'em over just to make her feel better."

"What's important is that we have the tickets and we'll soon be on the train. It's a good thing you knew something of the Penders family and their relations, so that our story would sound true."

"A cousin of mine punched cattle for Penders for a while," said Myra. "I remember him telling me about the spread. Look, there's the train."

The train in question was sitting on the tracks next to the freight shed, taking on water from the elevated tank. Bridget was waiting nearby, holding the reins of all three horses. Myra and Timothea moved over to join her and took their saddlebags off their mounts. Inside were the guns they would need later.

Myra caught hold of Bridget's hand and squeezed it. "See you later," she said.

"I'll be there," promised Bridget. "I'll get ahead of the train and wait at that arroyo you told me about."

Myra nodded. "Yep. That's where we'll make our move."

Longarm's horse picked its way carefully down the steep side of the dry wash. The sandy, pebble-littered bottom of the arroyo looked as if it hadn't seen any water in a month of Sundays, but Longarm knew that was deceptive. Out here, what was a roaring flood one day could be a muddy, stagnant trickle the next day and then utterly vanished the day after that.

As he reached the bottom of the wash, Longarm turned his head to look up at the railroad trestle some ten feet above his head. His eyes scanned the support beams and the underside of the structure. More than one bunch of outlaws had stopped a train by dynamiting just such a trestle. As far as he knew,

Myra and her friends didn't have any dynamite, but he wouldn't put anything past that redheaded catamount.

The trestle was clear, Longarm decided. He reined in and swung down from the saddle in order to lead his horse up the western bank of the arroyo. That made it easier on the animal.

When he reached the top, he paused and looked down at the ground. Three sets of fairly recent hoofprints were plain to see in the dust. They followed the railroad tracks until they reached the arroyo, then turned sharply and headed south, paralleling the dry wash.

Myra, Bridget, and Timothea, mused Longarm. That made three. But were they the same three as the ones who had left these tracks?

There was no way of knowing without following the trail along the arroyo, and as a distant roar came to Longarm's ears, he knew he didn't have time to do that.

The train was coming.

Longarm glanced at the sun. He estimated the time at a little after three o'clock. Once the eastbound reached this spot, at full speed it could make it to Van Horn in a little over half an hour, he figured. The train was not only on schedule, it was even a little early today.

Longarm mounted up and heeled the horse into a trot that carried it along beside the railroad tracks. His eyes followed the twin rails of steel as thcy dwindled and seemingly converged in the distance. A small black dot appeared at that apparent convergence. Puffs of white smoke billowed into the air. The dot quickly grew larger and resolved itself into the front end of a Baldwin locomotive, complete with diamond stack and cowcatcher. Longarm brought the horse to a halt and hurriedly dismounted.

He didn't have anything else to use as a flag, so he unpinned his badge, tucked it away, and hastily peeled off his shirt. He stepped over the rail and onto the roadbed and began to wave the white garment back and forth over his head.

The engineer probably had a habit of not watching too closely on this long, flat, straight stretch of track, so it was several seconds before he noticed the man standing in front of the train. The locomotive's whistle blew, so loud and shrill that the noise probably carried for several miles in the clear air. Longarm ignored the warning, stayed where he was, and kept waving the shirt over his head.

It occurred to him that the engineer might not stop because he was afraid that Longarm was a bandit. But the men in the locomotive's cab would be able to see he was alone as well, not another soul to be seen within half a mile.

Longarm had a nervous couple of seconds as the train kept barreling on down the tracks, but then he heard the squeal of brakes. With a visible shudder of the locomotive, the train began to slow down.

Longarm stayed where he was as the distance between him and the train dropped to a hundred yards, fifty, twenty-five. He was about to say the hell with it and fling himself off the tracks when the locomotive finally jolted to a halt about ten yards in front of him.

Shrugging back into his shirt, Longarm ran alongside the locomotive until he reached the cab. Both the engineer and the fireman were staring suspiciously at him. The fireman was clutching his coal shovel as if ready to clout somebody over the head with it.

Longarm left his gun holstered and reached for the wallet containing his badge and identification papers. He raised his voice so he could be heard over the banked rumble and hiss of the locomotive and called out, "I'm a lawman! Deputy U.S. marshal!" He tossed his bona fides up to the engineer.

The man caught the wallet, opened it, and studied the badge and papers, showing them to the fireman after a moment. Finally he nodded and extended a hand down to Longarm.

When he had climbed up into the cab, Longarm finished buttoning his shirt and tucked it back into his trousers. "Had any trouble since you left Sierra Blanca?" he asked.

The engineer shook his head. "Nary a bit. We been high-ballin' along just fine."

The fireman put in proudly, "Quarter-hour ahead o' schedule."

"I've got an idea that some owlhoots are going to try to

153

stop you and hold you up somewhere between here and Van Horn," said Longarm. He didn't mention anything about the owlhoots in question being women. The story was hard enough to believe without adding that.

The engineer looked skeptical. "Why in blazes would anybody want to do that? We're not carryin' anything except the normal run of passengers and freight."

Longarm hesitated only a second before saying, "You've got a strongbox full of cash, bound for the bank in Van Horn from the Federal Reserve in El Paso. It's probably back in the caboose with the conductor."

The engineer's frown deepened, and for a moment Longarm thought he wasn't convinced. But then the man burst out, "Damn that Curry!"

"Who's Curry?" asked Longarm.

"Conductor on this train. He don't never tell us nothin' about things like this! I wish him and the railroad and them government bankers in El Paso would quit hatchin' up these schemes."

The fireman said, "Curry's a close-mouthed sumbitch, all right."

"What do you want me to do, Marshal?" asked the engineer. "I can't very well back up all the way to Sierra Blanca, and we got a schedule to keep, too. They'll be expectin' us in Van Horn." He made a face. "We won't be ahead of time anymore, what with all this jawin'."

During the ride out here from Van Horn, Longarm had considered what to do if he intercepted the train before Myra and the others tried to stop it. Now he said, "I'll fetch my rifle from my horse and ride up here in the cab with you. I reckon if anybody does try to stop the train, they'll be in for a surprise."

He hoped he wouldn't be forced to kill any of the women. But he wasn't going to let Myra steal that strongbox full of cash, either.

The engineer nodded. "We'll get the old girl fired up while you're gettin' your Winchester." He turned to the fireman. "Let's get busy."

154

Longarm hopped down from the cab and went to his horse. He withdrew the Winchester from the saddle boot and then slapped the animal on the rump, sending it trotting back toward Van Horn. The horse would return to the settlement. Longarm would try to eventually get it back to Sheriff Ed Gray. If that wasn't possible, Billy Vail might have to honor an expense voucher for the animal. Longarm was sure Gray would put a high price on the horse.

As Longarm turned toward the locomotive, he saw a man in a dark blue suit and a billed cap stalking along beside the train. That would be the conductor, thought Longarm, coming to see why the train had made this unscheduled stop.

"Who the hell are you?" the conductor asked as he came up to Longarm, looking warily at the rifle in the lawman's hand.

"Deputy U.S. Marshal Custis Long. I'm here to make sure nobody wide-loops that strongbox you've got back in the caboose, old son."

The look of surprise in Curry's eyes told Longarm that he had guessed correctly about the location of the strongbox. "What . . . how . . ." the conductor stammered.

"It's a long story, and I don't yet have the straight of everything myself," Longarm told him. "For now, why don't you just get back in the caboose and tell whoever's guarding that box to stay awake. There might still be trouble between here and Van Horn."

Curry opened and closed his mouth a couple of times, then nodded. "All right, Marshal. But you'd better be telling the truth about who you are."

"I was last time I checked," Longarm said dryly. He went over to the cab and climbed up using the high metal step and the grab bar.

"What was Curry yammerin' about?" asked the engineer.

"He just wanted to know who I was and why the train was stopped. I was right about him having the strongbox in the caboose, by the way."

The engineer nodded. "Figured as much. Curry wouldn't want to let it out of his sight any more than necessary."

155

He eased the throttle forward, and with only a slight lurch, the locomotive's drivers engaged and sent the massive engine rolling ahead.

Longarm stood to one side, out of the way as the fireman fed coal into the engine. The train began to pick up speed, the junctions of the rails clacking past beneath the wheels. Longarm saw the horse he had ridden out here still trotting back toward Van Horn.

Within a few minutes, the train was approaching the trestle over the arroyo. Longarm felt his belly tensing as the locomotive neared the bridge. Everything still looked fine, no sign of any trouble.

Then the engineer called out, "Who in blazes are those fellas? More of your men, Marshal?"

The engineer was leaning out the window, peering ahead. The train clattered over the trestle, and Longarm felt the change as it began climbing the long grade on the other side of the dry wash. Longarm stepped over to the open side of the cab and held the Winchester in his right hand while he used his left to brace himself by grasping the grab bar.

Suddenly, the engineer grunted and stumbled backward, crashing into Longarm. The impact knocked Longarm toward the edge of the cab. With no more warning than that, he swung outward, his boots on the verge of slipping off into empty air. Only his grip on the grab bar kept him from plunging off the train.

Chapter 18

Longarm hung on for dear life.

His fingers were like iron as they clamped around the grab bar. The wind generated by the train's speed pummeled his face. Squinting against it, he looked back into the cab and saw the engineer sprawled on his back, a large, bloody stain spreading across the front of his bib overalls. The only conclusion Longarm could draw was that the engineer had been shot.

And as he turned to look up ahead of the train, he saw who had fired that fatal bullet.

The slug could have come from any of the four men galloping on horseback toward the train. They rode at breakneck speed down the slope from the top of the grade, racing alongside the tracks. All of them were shooting, puffs of smoke geysering from the muzzles of their rifles. As a bullet spanged off the outside of the locomotive's cab, not far from Longarm, he realized what a perfect target he was, hanging out there like that.

The corded muscles of his left arm and shoulder bunched as he heaved himself back into the cab. He almost stumbled over the body of the engineer but caught himself in time to keep from sprawling onto the iron flooring.

The fireman stared in horror at the bloody corpse of his partner. He didn't look up until Longarm shouted at him, "Can you run this engine?"

The fireman jerked his head in a nod. "Well enough to keep her on the tracks," he said.

"Then do it," ordered Longarm. While the fireman moved to take the throttle, Longarm went to the window and cautiously peered out. The bullet that had killed the engineer had been a lucky shot, no doubt about that; any bullet fired from the back of a running horse that actually found its target was well-nigh miraculous. But Longarm didn't want to chance lightning striking twice.

The riders were close now and still shooting. Longarm snapped the Winchester to his shoulder and pressed the trigger. The rifle cracked and bucked against his shoulder. The locomotive platform made a steadier platform to aim from than the hurricane deck of a saddle, so Longarm's shot was rewarded with the sight of one of the men swaying backward and toppling off his horse. The would-be train robber thudded limply to the ground, raising a small cloud of dust.

Who in blazes were these hombres? Longarm wondered. Something about one of them was vaguely familiar, but Longarm couldn't see him well enough through the dust and smoke and cinders to recognize him. They sure as hell weren't Myra and Bridget and Timothea, though.

Time enough to ponder such questions after he'd killed them, Longarm decided. He worked the lever of the Winchester and laid his cheek along the smooth wood of the stock to aim another shot.

What felt like a giant fist slammed into the side of his face. Longarm staggered back from the window, the rifle falling from his hands. At first he thought he'd been shot in the head, but then he saw the bent and damaged barrel of the Winchester and knew that a bullet had hit the rifle. That impact had slammed the stock against his cheek, stunning him. He shook his head, trying to clear away the cobwebs.

The Winchester was useless now. Longarm didn't even bother bending to retrieve it. He was reaching for his Colt when the fireman yelled a warning. "Look out, Marshal!"

One of the outlaws had turned his horse as he met the train so that he was now riding alongside the locomotive. Climbing the long grade had slowed the engine to the point that a horse could keep up with it. The outlaw had reached over and caught hold of the grab bar, and now, in a daring move, he kicked free of the stirrups and leaned out of the saddle, swinging his legs toward the train so that he landed inside the cab.

For one of the few times in Longarm's life, he was so surprised that he froze with his fingers wrapped around the butt of his gun. Staring at him from across the cab was an all-too-familiar face.

"Gray!"

"Long!"

The exclamations came from both men. Longarm was a little more shocked to see the sheriff from Fort Stockton than Gray was to see him, though, so that gave Gray the split-second of advantage he needed to fling himself across the cab. Gray tackled Longarm around the waist, pinning his gun hand, and the collision drove Longarm back against the far wall of the cab.

As he struggled with Gray, Longarm realized that the sheriff had crossed over the line from corruption to outright banditry. The only reason Gray could be here was to steal that strongbox.

The train slowed even more. With the fireman at the throttle, no one was feeding coal into the firebox. That meant the engine was losing power, and coupled with the grade it was climbing, the loss was becoming serious. If the train came to a stop, Gray's remaining two partners, whoever they were, would have no trouble boarding the cab and helping Gray finish off Longarm.

Those thoughts flashed through Longarm's brain as he braced himself and shoved Gray toward the front of the cab. Gray's back struck the closed door of the firebox. The fiery touch of the superheated metal seared through Gray's vest and shirt and tore a scream from his throat. Longarm swung a hard left fist that smashed into Gray's jaw and closed his mouth. He followed it with a short, sharp right that rocked Gray's head back.

"Marshal—"

The thud of boots on the iron floor of the cab was followed immediately by the roar of a gun. Longarm jerked around to see that a tall man in a black frock coat had also climbed into the cab from horseback. Powder-smoke curled from the muzzle of the man's gun barrel. The fireman sagged against the throttle, bent over and clutching his belly. The man who had shot him swung his gun toward Longarm.

This time there was no hesitation on the lawman's part. His hand flashed with blinding speed to the holstered gun in the cross-draw rig. Still, no matter how fast Longarm's draw was, he couldn't beat a man with a gun already in his hand.

The outlaw's Colt blasted first, followed less than a heartbeat later by the crash of Longarm's gun. The man in the black frock coat hurried his shot a little more than was necessary, however, and his bullet whipped harmlessly past Longarm's head. The slug from Longarm's gun drove into the outlaw's chest and flung him backward. The man made a futile, instinctive grab for something to hang on to, but he vanished as he fell out of the cab.

Longarm didn't have time to savor the triumph. With a roar of rage, Gray enveloped him from behind, wrapping his arms around Longarm in a crushing bear hug.

Both of them almost went out of the cab as Longarm staggered toward the edge. He jerked up his left leg at the last second and slammed the sole of his boot against the wall of the cab, stopping them. A hard shove with his leg sent them stumbling back in the other direction.

It was a deadly dance they performed there in the cab of the locomotive. As Longarm struggled with Gray, he saw that the wounded fireman had picked himself up and was again clinging to the throttle, trying to keep the train going as long as possible. The man was gutshot and probably doomed, but he wasn't giving up. Neither was Longarm.

Gray's left arm came up and locked underneath Longarm's neck, cutting off his air. Longarm grimaced as he fought for breath. Gray's right arm was still looped around him, pinning Longarm's right arm so that he couldn't bring his gun into play. Longarm twisted, fighting to get his feet braced against

160

the floor of the cab, then thrust hard with his legs, forcing Gray toward the door of the firebox once more.

With his back already badly burned, Gray wanted to avoid slamming into the firebox door again. His grip on Longarm loosened as he struggled to avoid that fate. Longarm was able to drive his left elbow back into Gray's midsection. That made Gray's hold on him slip even more.

Longarm tore free and whirled around. The gun in his hand smashed against the side of Gray's head. The crooked sheriff sagged toward the floor of the cab. He grabbed weakly at Longarm, but Longarm brought his knee up and slammed it into Gray's face. Gray went over backward, arms flung wide, out cold as he landed on the floor of the cab.

Where the hell was the fourth and final member of Gray's bandit crew? Longarm had recognized the man in the frock coat as a former member of the posse, and he figured the others were, too. Gray must have recruited the ones he knew he could trust to help him with this attempted robbery, then split off from the rest of the posse with some sort of excuse.

Longarm didn't see the fourth man. Could be the fella had realized how much of a fight Longarm was putting up and decided to abandon the plan to hold up the train. Keeping his gun drawn and ready, Longarm sprang to the side of the fireman, who was still clutching the throttle bar.

"Can you make it, old son?" Longarm asked the man.

The fireman nodded. His face was pale and covered with beads of sweat, and his eyes were big with the pain that filled his body. But determination and courage shone there as well.

"Gonna have to have . . . some more coal," he grated between clenched teeth. "Take my . . . gloves. . . . Once we . . . reach the top of the grade . . . we'll pick up speed again."

Longarm holstered his gun, reluctant to do so but knowing that the fireman was right. He pulled the thick gloves off the man's hands one at a time, so that the fireman always had one hand on the throttle. Longarm yanked the gloves on, picked up the shovel, and jerked open the firebox door.

The roaring blaze inside had died down considerably. Longarm turned to the coal tender, rammed the shovel through the opening into the pile of black, bituminous lumps. He turned, took a long stride that carried him across the cab, and flung the shovelful of coal into the firebox. He did that again and again, and with the third shovelful of coal he saw that the flames inside the box had begun to leap higher.

For several minutes, Longarm fed coal to the firebox. The engine, which had been struggling to keep the train moving up the incline, began to throb with added power. The train's speed picked up slightly. Longarm glanced out the window, saw that the top of the grade was approaching.

Looked like they were going to make it after all.

"Where the hell do you think you're going?" asked Timothea, grabbing at the sleeve of Myra's dress as the redhead began to clamber over the railing around the open platform at the front of the passenger car.

Myra tried to pull loose. "We've got to get up to the cab, so we can stop the train."

"Then what?" demanded Timothea. "That strongbox is probably in the caboose. You said so yourself. Even if you manage to climb up to the cab and stop the train, how will we get the money then?"

Myra frowned. Damn it, Timothea was right, she admitted to herself. At one time, Myra had wanted to get shed of all the other prisoners who'd escaped from the wagon with her and Bridget, but Timothea was proving herself to be mighty useful. Maybe when this was over and all that money was theirs, they could stay together and plan some other job.

"You're right," Myra said as she swung her leg back over the railing onto the platform. "It'd be better to get into the caboose and stop the train from there. Bridget can still catch up."

"Can we do that? Stop the train from the caboose, I mean?"

Myra nodded. "The conductor's got an emergency cord he can pull. That'll do the trick. All we have to do is take care of the guards and the conductor."

Timothea smiled and said, "That shouldn't be a problem for us."

Myra reached for the door leading back into the passenger car. "Come on."

The two of them had gotten a few curious looks from the other passengers when they stepped out onto the forward platform and closed the door behind them. Now they were on the receiving end of more stares as they reentered the car and made their way along the aisle toward the rear door. Let these yokels think whatever they want, Myra told herself. Pretty soon it wouldn't matter. Pretty soon she and her companions would be famous all across West Texas as the bunch who had pulled the most daring robbery since the James boys.

The train was fairly short, only one passenger car, four freight cars, and the caboose. As Myra and Timothea stood on the rear platform of the passenger car, Timothea looked stricken and asked, "How do we get to the caboose?"

"Same way I was going to get to the engine," said Myra. "Up and over."

Iron bars were set into the end of the freight car to be used as a ladder. Myra climbed over the platform railing, clinging tightly to it with one hand as she reached for the nearest of the bars with the other. She tried to ignore the sight of the roadbed streaking past less than a yard below her feet. She had to lean out away from the platform to grab hold of one of the bars. When she had a good grip, she let go with her other hand and used it to grab a second bar. Her feet swung free, dangling for a long second before she managed to get them on one of the lower bars.

She looked back over her shoulder at a pale-faced Timothea and yelled over the rattle of the train's passage, "Come on!"

Timothea just shook her head.

"It's not as hard as it looks!" Myra assured her. "Just don't look down! Come on, damn it!"

She started to climb toward the roof of the freight car. When she glanced back, she saw that Timothea still hadn't budged.

"All right, then!" Myra shouted angrily. "I'll just take all the money for me and Bridget!"

That seemed to get through to Timothea's fear-stricken brain. She took a deep breath, then climbed awkwardly over

163

the platform railing. There was barely enough room outside the railing for the toes of her shoes. She swallowed hard, let go with one hand, and reached for the nearest bar on the wall of the freight car.

Myra was at the top by this time. She pulled herself onto the roof of the car, then turned so that she could look back down into the space between the cars. She saw that Timothea had managed to get hold of the bars and was climbing slowly. Myra nodded encouragement and then reached out to grasp Timothea's arm and help pull her onto the roof.

Timothea sprawled out, shaking and gulping down deep breaths. Myra sat beside her and said, "It's too hard clambering around these cars in these damned long dresses. I'm getting rid of mine." She started ripping away the skirt of the dress.

A moment later, Timothea sat up and followed suit. They tossed the discarded skirts over the side of the freight car. That left them in the denim trousers they had worn under the dresses.

Myra stood up, holding her arms out to the side to balance herself. "Let's go," she said. She started toward the rear of the freight car at a careful walk. Timothea followed a little more slowly, her face still etched with the pallor of fear.

When they reached the end of the car, Myra said, "We can either climb down and try to reach across for the ladder on the other car, or we can jump."

"J-jump?" repeated Timothea. She stared at the six-foot gap between cars.

"We can do it," said Myra, sounding confident even though she had never even attempted such a thing. "The train's going one way, and we'll be jumping the other way. So it'll meet us more than halfway."

"You're sure about this?"

"I don't see any other way to do it."

Timothea swallowed and nodded. "All right then. You go first."

"Sure." Needing no more encouragement than that, Myra backed off a few feet, broke into a run, and leaped off the end of the freight car. She sailed into the air, clearing the gap easily, and landed feet-first on top of the next car. She stumbled, went to her knees, caught herself. Then she turned and motioned for Timothea to come on.

Timothea pushed back the hair that the wind was whipping into her face. Without pausing too long to think about what she was doing, she took a running start as Myra had done and jumped the gap between cars. Myra caught her, and both women fell to the roof of the car. They were in the center, however, so there was little danger of them sliding off.

Myra picked herself up and brushed herself off. "Come on," she said with a grin. "Just two more to go."

Timothea sighed and rolled her eyes, but she followed Myra to the end of this car.

It took only a few minutes to negotiate the other two freight cars in the same manner. When they reached the end of the final car, the platform of the caboose loomed beneath them as their next destination.

"We'll jump down there from up here," decided Myra.

"You're sure about this?"

"Haven't steered you wrong yet, have I?"

Timothea didn't answer that. She just said, "Let's do it."

A moment later, two sets of feet thudded onto the platform, one right after the other. Myra caught hold of Timothea's arm to steady her. "You ready?" she asked.

"Give me a minute." Timothea drew in several deep breaths, then nodded. "All right."

Both women reached under the blouses of their dresses and pulled out the six-guns they had hidden there. Myra held her gun down beside her leg so that it wasn't readily visible, then pounded on the door of the caboose with her other hand. "Help, please help!" she cried as loudly as she could. "Bandits! Help!"

A second later the door was jerked open, and an astonished-looking man in a blue suit peered out at them. "My God!" he exclaimed. "How did you ladies get back here? And what was that about bandits?"

"They're right here," Myra said coolly as she brought up

her gun and shoved the barrel against the conductor's chest, forcing him backward into the caboose.

The two guards were taken by surprise as much as the conductor was. They had been playing cards, but they had their shotguns in their hands now, alerted to the possibility of trouble by the pounding on the door. Still, they had no chance to bring the weapons to bear before Timothea stepped past Myra and leveled her pistol at them. "Don't move," she said sharply.

The conductor's mouth was opening and closing like he was a fish on dry land. "What . . . what . . ." he managed to say.

Myra slashed the gun across his face, knocking him backward. "We're helping ourselves to that strongbox you've got back here," she said. Then she glanced up, spotted what she was looking for, and reached for the emergency cord.

One of the guards tried to jerk his shotgun up. Timothea had him covered, but she hesitated. Myra saw the flicker of movement from the corner of her eye and pivoted toward the guards, opening up with the Colt as she did so. Her first slug smashed into the chest of the guard who had tried to use his scattergun. The man went over backward in his chair as his finger clenched involuntarily on both triggers. The twin barrels of the greener erupted with flame and lead, but the charges went harmlessly into the ceiling. Myra kept firing, sending the second guard spinning to the floor of the caboose, the front of his shirt already heavily stained with blood.

Timothea gaped at the bodies of the guards. "You . . . you killed them!"

"It was them or us," Myra said. Inside, she was shaking, but she was damned if she would show it.

Her hand was rock-steady as she reached up to the emergency cord, grasped it, and pulled down hard.

Chapter 19

Longarm was thrown off his feet as the train suddenly lurched to a stop. Its brakes howled against the steel rails with a sound like that of a demented banshee. Longarm landed on top of the unconscious Sheriff Ed Gray and then rolled off the crooked lawman. The fireman had been jolted forward against the throttle. Now he fell backward, his stubborn strength finally deserting him. The belly of his overalls was sodden with blood.

Longarm pushed himself upright and stepped to the edge of the cab. Something had stopped the train about a hundred yards short of the crest of the rise, and it sure as hell hadn't been him. Maybe the conductor had pulled the emergency cord back in the caboose. Longarm had no idea why Curry would have done that; the caboose was clear at the other end of the train, and Curry shouldn't have had any idea that all Hades was breaking loose up in the cab.

Suddenly, Longarm had a feeling he knew where that fourth outlaw had gone.

He wheeled around, went to the other side of the cab, and leaped down to the ground. Using the train itself to shield him from any prying eyes, he ran along it toward the caboose. Gun in hand, he paused as he neared the rear end of the last freight car. He could see the door of the caboose now, could see that

167

it was standing open. A faint smell of burnt powder came to his nose.

Yep, there had been trouble back here, too.

Moving carefully and quietly, Longarm crouched and cat-footed along the length of the caboose until he reached its rear platform. Whoever was inside wouldn't be expecting any problem to come from that direction. He pulled himself up onto the platform and braced himself, then lifted his right leg and drove the heel of his boot against the door, just above the knob. The door slammed open and Longarm was through it in an instant, gun leveled. "Hold it!" he yelled.

For the second time this afternoon, he got a hell of a surprise. Myra and Timothea, wearing trousers and what looked like the top half of some dresses, were pulling a heavy strong-box toward the front door of the caboose. A couple of dead men were sprawled on the floor, and the train's conductor lay either unconscious or dead near the wall, his face bloody from a long, ragged gash in his forehead.

"Long!" Myra gasped. Her pistol was tucked behind her belt, and her hand began to stray toward the butt.

Longarm glared over the sights of his Colt. "Don't do it," he said coldly. "I don't want to kill you, lady, but I'll damned sure do it if I have to."

He still didn't know where the last of the men who had been with Gray had gotten off to, nor could he account for Bridget. But it was obvious that Myra and Timothea had gotten into the caboose somehow, killed the guards and maybe the conductor, and had been in the process of stealing the strongbox full of cash when Longarm interrupted them.

"I don't reckon it'd be any use trying to strike a bargain, would it?" said Myra.

"No use at all," Longarm told her grimly. "Now, use your left hands and take those guns out, slow and careful-like. . . ."

He heard the gun go off behind him, but there was nothing he could do about it. Something crashed into his left side, turning him halfway around. He grunted in pain as he started to fall. Myra leaped forward, her foot lashing out in a savage kick. The toe of her boot caught Longarm on the wrist and knocked the gun from his fingers.

Myra stepped back and jerked her gun out. A smile of triumph lit her face. Longarm looked up at her, grimacing from the pain in his side and expecting her to empty her Colt into him at any second. Instead she glanced past him and let out a whoop of exultation as hoofbeats sounded behind the train. "A hell of a shot, Bridget!" she yelled in congratulations.

Bridget. Longarm had wondered about her, but he hadn't gotten around yet to checking on her whereabouts. Now he was paying the price for that lack of time.

"Cover the marshal," Myra snapped at Timothea, who had also drawn her gun. Myra tucked her own away and bent to grab hold of the handle on the end of the strongbox. She dragged it toward the rear door. "Give me a hand!" she called to Bridget. "We've got to get out of here before any of the passengers work up the nerve to come see what's happening."

Bridget hurried into the caboose, stepping past Longarm's fallen form. He gritted his teeth and tried to summon up the strength to make a move, but to no avail. He was fairly sure the wound in his side wasn't too serious; more than likely the slug had just plowed a shallow furrow in him. But it was bleeding pretty heavily, and the shock of the injury had stolen all his strength.

Damned if after all this he was going to let those women get away with that money, he told himself. *Damned if he was.*

"You bitches!"

The rage-filled shout came from the front of the caboose. It was still echoing when a gun blasted. Bridget had bent over to pick up one end of the strongbox, and she kept bending as she grunted in pain. She came up on her toes and collapsed over the strongbox as Myra screamed her name.

Longarm's head snapped around and he saw Timothea turn toward the front of the caboose, gun in hand. More shots crashed, and she staggered back a step. But her gun was roaring, too, flame lancing from the muzzle as she jerked the trigger. The bullets thudded into the chest of Sheriff Ed Gray and forced him back out of the open doorway. The railing at the

169

edge of the platform stopped him as Timothea continued to empty her Colt into him. Gray dropped his own gun and hung there against the railing for a second before pitching forward onto his face. He fell half-in, half-out of the door into the caboose.

"Thea!" Myra said urgently.

Timothea turned away from the man she had just killed. Her face was ashen, and Longarm saw blood on her dress. But she was still on her feet and her steps were steady as she holstered her gun and went to Myra.

Myra's face was wet with tears. "Bridget's dead," she said in a ragged voice as she looked up at Timothea.

"We all will be if we don't get out of here," said Timothea. Getting shot at had somehow put steel in her voice and in her backbone. "Come on. We'll tie the strongbox to Bridget's horse and drag it. That's what you were planning to do, wasn't it?"

"Y-yeah. I reckon." Myra wiped her sleeve across her face as she came to her feet. She pulled her gun and turned toward Longarm. "But first—"

"No." Timothea's voice was sharp, commanding. "There's no need for anybody else to die. Marshal Long was just doing his job."

"But Bridget—"

"It was that other man who shot her. Killing the marshal won't bring her back."

For a second, Longarm thought Myra was going to shoot him anyway. Then she sighed, thrust the gun behind her belt again, and bent to grab the strongbox. "You're right," she said to Timothea. "Come on."

Between them, the two women wrestled the strongbox onto the platform. Myra went to Bridget's horse and came back with a rope. Quickly, she tied it to one of the handles, then went back to secure the other end to the saddlehorn. "Ready," she announced.

Timothea looked down at Longarm. "We spared your life, Marshal," she said. "Don't come after us again."

Longarm met the eyes with which she so coolly regarded him, and he said, "You know better."

"Maybe." A bleak smile touched her lips. "But there's still been enough killing."

She turned and jumped down from the platform. A moment later, Longarm heard the rattle of hooves as several horses broke into a trot. The strongbox disappeared as the rope grew taut and pulled it off the platform.

Longarm tasted bitter defeat in his mouth. He looked across the caboose at Bridget, who still lay where she had fallen after she rolled off the strongbox. Her face was slack, her sightless eyes open.

She and Myra had wanted to be famous outlaws. Well, Bridget would never achieve that goal. Myra still might, though, if she and Timothea got away with that strongbox.

Longarm began to push himself to his feet. If he could just find a horse somewhere, maybe one of those ridden by Gray and his companions. . . .

What little strength he had ran out of him like water. Longarm fell again, jolting hard against the floor of the caboose and seeming to fall all the way through it into yawning blackness.

He came back to consciousness an unknowable time later. His shirt was stiff with dried blood and his side ached intolerably. But tolerate it he did, pushing himself into a sitting position with a grunt of effort.

"Don't move!" someone ordered.

Longarm looked around, saw several men who could only be some of the passengers. A couple of them, cattlemen by the looks of them, held revolvers.

"I'm a U.S. marshal," Longarm said tiredly. He held up his arm. "Somebody give me a hand."

One of the men took his hand and helped him to his feet. Longarm shook his head in an attempt to clear away some of the cobwebs. Another of the men said, "What in tarnation happened back here? The train stopped for some reason, and we heard shooting, and when we came back here it looked like a damned slaughterhouse.''

"Bodies everywhere," added the man who had helped Longarm up. "We thought you were dead at first, too, Marshal."

"Can you prove you're who you say you are?" asked a third man.

Longarm ignored the question and asked one of his own. "How long has the train been stopped?"

"Twenty, maybe twenty-five minutes," replied one of the men.

That meant Myra and Timothea had a lead of at least fifteen minutes, thought Longarm. He might still be able to catch up to them if he could get his hands on a horse. He started toward the door, still ignoring the questions that the passengers threw at him.

Before he could reach the opening, a new figure appeared in it. The man was tall and broad-shouldered, with long, sandy hair under his hat. He put up a hand to stop Longarm and said, "Hold on there, mister. Where do yo think you're going?"

"After the outlaws who stole a strongbox full of cash from this caboose," grated Longarm. "I'm a federal marshal. Now get the hell out of my way!"

The stranger smiled slightly. "No need to get your back up, Marshal. Maybe we can help each other out. It just so happens I'm a lawman, too. Constable Pete Durrell from Van Horn."

"Van Horn . . . ?" repeated Longarm. He was still a little dizzy.

"That's right. I'm after a bunch of female owlhoots who robbed the bank there." Durrell nodded toward Bridget's body. "Reckon she must be one of them. Was it the others who got away with the loot from this train?"

Longarm nodded. "Two of 'em, anyway. The last two."

"Well, then, what say we go after them together?" suggested Durrell. "After you get that bullet hole in your side patched up."

"There's no time—"

"Better have it looked after now, otherwise you'll be liable

172

to pass out and slow us down even more, Marshal.''

Durrell's words made sense, Longarm decided. He grunted and started to sit down on a bench, then changed his mind and stepped out onto the platform. The smell of freshly-spilled blood was too strong for him to stay in the caboose another minute. He dragged a breath of fresh air into his lungs and felt a little better immediately.

There wasn't a doctor among the passengers, but several men had experience patching up bullet wounds, a skill acquired by most men who stayed alive for very long on the frontier. Longarm peeled off his blood-soaked shirt and saw that he had been right about the wound: It was just a crease along his ribs. He could tell from the lack of pain when he breathed deeply that none of the bones were broken or even cracked. One of the passengers dug a flask of whiskey from a coat pocket, soaked a cloth with the fiery stuff, and swabbed away the dried blood. A sharply indrawn breath hissed in Longarm's nostrils as the man cleaned the wound itself with the whiskey.

''Here,'' the man said as he handed the flask to Longarm. ''A slug of this who-hit-John will probably help your insides, too.''

Longarm agreed with that. He tipped up the flask and took a long swallow. The whiskey burned all the way down to his belly, but the fire gave him more strength.

One of the men went up to the passenger car and came back with a spare shirt and several strips of cloth torn from the hem of a lady's petticoat. ''My wife was glad to make the contribution,'' he said with a grin.

The man who was doctoring Longarm soaked another pad with whiskey, then tied it in place over the wound. He wrapped the other strips of cloth around Longarm's torso, making sure the bandage would remain where it was supposed to be. ''You ought to sit down and rest for a while, Marshal,'' he advised.

Longarm shook his head. ''Can't. Durrell and I got to go after those women.''

One of the men shook his head and said, "Lady bandits. If that don't beat all."

Myra probably would have been pleased to hear the awe in the man's voice, thought Longarm.

He got into the clean shirt, found his Colt on the floor of the caboose and holstered it. Another quarter-hour had passed since he regained consciousness. Myra and Timothea would have a good lead. But they were dragging that strongbox, and that would slow them down. Longarm nodded to Durrell and said, "Let's go."

"I found an extra horse you can ride, Marshal," the constable said. "Don't know where it came from, but you know what they say about gift horses."

The animal had been Gray's; Longarm recognized it. But that part of the story was too long and complicated to go into. He took the reins from Durrell and swung up in the saddle, feeling only a slight twinge from his tightly bandaged side as he did so.

"Come on," Longarm said. "We've got us some outlaws to catch."

Chapter 20

Ginny's hips pumped back and forth frenziedly as she rode on Reuben's shaft. He lay flat on his back in the bed while she straddled his hips and did most of the work, since he was still recuperating from his wound. Loving was just about the best medicine a fella could have, Ginny knew, and she planned to give Reuben plenty of it.

She sat straight up so that he was as deep in her as he could go. His hands cupped and squeezed her breasts. She bit her bottom lip as she thrust at him. Her hands rested on his chest, her fingers pulling lightly at his nipples.

The thick pole of male flesh throbbed and swelled within her. Ginny knew he was about to come, and that knowledge sent her spinning over the edge of her own climax. She cried out as he began to spurt inside her.

When they were both drained, Ginny sagged forward, lying on Reuben's chest and pillowing her head on his shoulder. His gradually softening manhood was still buried within her. He stroked her hair and her back and kissed her forehead. "It was the best day of my life when you showed up here, Ginny," he said quietly.

She lifted her head and smiled. "But you got shot."

"It was worth it, every bit."

She moved her head a few inches and kissed him, her lips brushing lightly over his. The kiss might have deepened into one more passionate, but suddenly Ginny lifted her head again. A wary look came over her face.

Reuben caught his breath. "I hear it, too," he said. "Hoof-beats. Riders coming."

Ginny rolled off him and reached for the dress she had draped over a chair beside the bunk. Reuben stood up and stepped into his trousers, then pulled his boots on. The Henry rifle was lying on the table. He picked it up as the hoofbeats came to a halt outside the cabin. Reuben's face was grim as he moved toward the door. If whoever had come to call wasn't friendly, they'd get a mighty hot welcome.

But before Reuben could reach the door, a woman's voice called out, "Hello the cabin!"

"Damn!" said Ginny. "That sounds like Myra."

She had pulled the dress over her head. Now she hurried to the door and yanked it open. Reuben was right behind her, the rifle held ready if he needed it.

Both of them saw quickly that there was no danger. Myra and Timothea sat on horseback in front of the cabin. Myra was leading a riderless horse. She looked dirty and tired, as if she had been riding for a long time. Timothea looked even worse. Her face was colorless, and she had to hold on tightly to the saddlehorn to stay on her mount.

"Can you give us a hand?" asked Myra. "Thea's been hurt."

Ginny sprang forward, reaching up as Timothea swayed in the saddle. "Reuben!" she said, and he leaned the Henry against the wall and hurried forward to help her. Together, they lifted Timothea down from the horse while Myra was swinging down from her mount.

"Let's take her inside," said Ginny. She looked at Myra. "What happened to her?"

"She was shot. It's a long story."

"And I'll bet it was because she was going along with one of your wild ideas."

Myra flushed angrily. "Just help her, damn it. I ain't in no mood to argue with you."

Ginny regretted the impulse that had led her to start poking

176

at the sore place between her and Myra right away. Myra was right: It was more important now that they tend to Timothea. Ginny and Reuben got her onto the bunk inside the cabin, then stepped back as Myra followed them in and dumped several saddlebags on the table. The pouches were bulging with whatever was inside them.

"Where's Bridget and Abigail and Deborah?" Ginny asked as she pulled back the blood-stained blouse Timothea was wearing.

"Bridget's dead," Myra replied dully. "I don't know where the other two are. In a jail cell somewhere, more than likely. They left us, ran off with a lawman we crossed trails with."

Ginny's jaw tightened. "I'm sorry to hear about Bridget," she said, and she found to her surprise that she meant it.

"Well, there's nothing can be done about it now." Myra's tone was cool, seemingly unfeeling, but Ginny knew better. She knew Myra had to be hurting.

Ginny's fingers moved quickly, laying bare the bullet hole in Timothea's side. It looked like the slug had punched in from the front and gone cleanly out the back. Crude bandages had been applied to the wounds, but Timothea had obviously lost quite a bit of blood, and the flesh around both bullet holes was red and swollen. Ginny laid a hand on the woman's forehead. Timothea was feverish, too.

Ginny shook her head. "It doesn't look too good. We've got to clean those wounds and try to get her fever down."

"I did the best I could," Myra said defensively. "Hell, I could've taken the money and rode off without her. I didn't have to bring her with me."

Ginny wondered what money Myra was talking about. That was probably what was bulging those saddlebags. "When did this happen?"

"A couple of days ago, up between Van Horn and Sierra Blanca."

"That's a long way to ride with a bullet wound."

"We didn't have much choice," Myra said flatly. "This was the closest place I could think of where we might be able to get some help."

"So you brought your trouble back here with you," said Reuben. His voice was tight and angry.

Myra snapped, "I told you, I didn't have any choice."

"You could have left Timothea to die," Ginny pointed out. "You said so yourself. I'm glad you didn't, but it's still a choice."

Myra shrugged. "We rode too many trails together, I reckon. Can you fix her up?"

"I'll do what I can," promised Ginny.

"Thanks." The word came out sullen and grudging. She couldn't really expect any more than that from Myra, Ginny told herself.

For the next hour, she worked over Timothea, cleaning and rebandaging the wounds, stripping off the filthy clothes, and rubbing a cool, wet cloth over the injured woman's body. Reuben went outside while Ginny was doing that, leaving Ginny and Myra alone. After a while, Ginny said, "You want to tell me about all of it?"

"You mean since we left here?"

"That's right."

Myra sighed and said, "Might as well, I guess. I figured we were going to make ourselves rich. . . ."

Longarm and Durrell had found the empty strongbox less than an hour after riding away from the stalled train.

"I was worried they'd think about doing that," said Longarm as he rested his hands on the saddlehorn and looked down at the strongbox with its bullet-destroyed lock. "They busted it open and split up the money between all the saddlebags they had."

"They can travel faster carrying it that way," said Durrell.

"Not fast enough or far enough."

Durrell grinned. "I like the way you think, Marshal."

They pushed on, following the tracks left by Myra and Timothea until the sun set and it grew too dark to read sign. Longarm supposed they could keep going, trusting luck to keep them on the trail, but he didn't want to chance that. Better a long chase that yielded results, he decided, than a shorter one that proved futile. Durrell agreed.

"We'll catch them," the constable from Van Horn said confidently. "It's just a matter of time."

They rode on as soon as it was light enough to see the next morning. Longarm estimated that they had lost ground during the night; Myra had probably insisted on riding after dark, though they would have had to stop eventually, if only to rest the horses. All day, Longarm and Durrell followed the tracks, losing the trail a time or two when it crossed rocky ground that wouldn't take hoofprints, but they were always able to pick it up again. One of the horses they were following had a nicked shoe, and that told the two lawmen they were still on the right track.

Longarm's side ached. He tried to ignore the pain and only checked the wound from time to time to make sure it hadn't started bleeding again. Durrell commented during the afternoon, "You must be a stubborn man, Marshal. Most gents would be laid up for a while after being shot, even if it was just a scratch like that one."

"That money belongs to Uncle Sam until it gets to the bank in Van Horn," replied Longarm. "I don't intend to let those women get away with it."

"Neither do I," said Durrell.

By nightfall, Longarm felt that they had closed the gap somewhat. "Myra's been pushing the horses too hard," he said. "They can't keep going like that."

"We ought to catch up with them tomorrow," speculated Durrell.

Longarm nodded in agreement and looked south toward the Davis Mountains. "Somewhere in those foothills, more than likely," he said, wondering if the rest of Gray's posse was still wandering around down there somewhere, too.

It seemed like a year since Longarm had had any hot food or coffee, but they pitched a cold camp again that night. Early the next morning, the two lawmen rode on. Some of the scenery was growing familiar to Longarm. He saw a line of green in the distance and wondered if it marked the course of Diablo Creek. He had a feeling it did.

By midday Longarm and Durrell had left the arid flatland behind them and were in the pine-dotted foothills. The trail was harder to follow now, but when Longarm was able to spot hoofprints, they looked pretty recent.

"Smoke up ahead," Durrell pointed out. "Probably from the chimney of a ranch house, by the looks of it."

Longarm agreed. "Those women may have stopped there. We'd best check it out." He knew Myra wouldn't balk at stealing fresh horses at gunpoint.

Half an hour later, they reined in at the top of a ridge and looked down into the shallow valley between two foothills. A double log cabin, a barn, and some corrals were down there. Longarm saw a man cross from the cabin to the barn. The rancher moved unhurriedly, as if he had nothing in the world to worry about.

Longarm's hackles rose anyway. Every instinct in his body warned him that things weren't as peaceful on this isolated ranch as they seemed at first glance.

"Let's circle around," he suggested, "check out that barn before we let anybody know we're here."

"Good idea," agreed Durrell. "Never hurts to be careful."

They dropped back down to the far side of the ridge and rode along it until it petered out. Skirting the cabin, they approached the barn from the rear. Longarm didn't know if the rancher was still in there or not, so when they got within earshot, he brought his horse to a stop and motioned for Durrell to do the same. They dismounted and tied the horses to a couple of saplings, then started forward on foot. Longarm drew his Colt, and Durrell brought his Winchester and held it canted across his chest, ready for use.

The barn's back door stood partially open. Longarm eased up to it and stopped to listen. The only sounds from inside the barn were the stampings and blowings of some horses and maybe a milk cow. After a moment, Longarm nodded to Durrell and then slipped inside.

It was dim inside the barn, but not so much so that Longarm couldn't see. The place was empty of humans. The rancher must have gone back inside the cabin while they were riding around the ridge, thought Longarm. He walked quietly over to the stalls where several horses stood munching on grain.

The animals moved around nervously at the approach of strangers, but they were quiet about it, a fact for which Long-arm was grateful.

His hand tightened on the butt of his Colt as he recognized three of the horses. "Those are the ones we've been follow-ing," he said quietly to Durrell. "Those gals have been here."

"Or they're still here," said Durrell.

"Yeah, could be."

"We've got to get into that cabin."

"Got any ideas?"

Durrell shrugged. "We could set it on fire, smoke 'em out."

"That rancher's probably in there, and he might have a family, too," said Longarm with a frown. "I don't cotton to burning down a man's home unless I have to."

"You said you wanted to get that money back and catch up to those women. Seemed to me like a good way to maybe do that."

"We'll find another way." Longarm thought about the problem for a moment, then said, "Give me a few minutes to get into position, then run these horses out of here. The sound of them stampeding ought to bring everybody in the cabin out into the open."

Durrell nodded. "Sounds like it might work. Where are you going to be?"

"Around on the other side of that cabin."

"Five minutes?"

"Ought to do it," said Longarm.

He left Durrell in the barn and went out the back. The rancher had cleared away most of the trees around the place, partially for the logs and partially so that intruders couldn't slip up on him too easily, thought Longarm. But there was enough cover for him to make his way unseen until he was about fifty yards from the cabin. He crouched behind a fallen log and waited.

Durrell did his part right on time. Longarm heard the sudden thunder of hoofbeats in the clearing between the cabin and the barn. Anyone inside the cabin must have heard the stampede, too. Longarm saw the horses, half a dozen of them, galloping off into the timber. He heard yells of alarm from the cabin.

Longarm came up out of his crouch and ran toward the cabin as fast as he could. He stopped at the corner and stuck his gun around it, his arm extended. "Hold it!" he yelled at the man who stood in the clearing. The man's back was to Longarm, but the lawman could tell that he was holding a Henry rifle. "Drop it!"

The man stiffened, and for a second Longarm thought he was going to spin around and shoot. But then Durrell called from the barn, "You're covered, mister!"

The man's shoulders slumped. He bent and put the rifle on the ground in front of him.

Longarm stepped past the corner of the cabin. As he did so, he saw a flicker of movement from the corner of his eye. He started to turn toward it, saw Myra step out of the cabin with a gun in her hand. She leveled it at him and said, "Drop your gun, Marshal."

Longarm's Colt was pointed halfway between the rancher and Myra. He could drop the rancher easily, but that would give Myra a clear shot at him. If he finished his turn and tried to take Myra, the rancher would have a chance to grab up his rifle and maybe take a hand in the shoot-out.

But that was probably the last thing on the man's mind. Likely he was just an innocent bystander in this fracas. Besides, Durrell was in the barn, and he could pick off the rancher if the man tried to interfere. Longarm took a deep breath.

"Put the gun down, Myra," he said. "Like Timothea said back at the train a couple of days ago, there's been enough killing."

Durrell stepped out of the barn. "No, not yet there hasn't," he said.

Longarm saw that Durrell's rifle was now pointed at *him*. What the hell—!

"Drop it, Long!" called Durrell. "Gray may not have killed you, but I sure as hell will."

Myra's eyes widened as she looked across the clearing. "Durrell!" she exclaimed.

"You know him?" asked Longarm.

"He was in the bank at Van Horn!" cried Myra. "He's the

one who killed those men—'' She jerked her gun away from Longarm and pointed it toward Durrell.

Time seemed to freeze for Longarm. He saw it all plain as day now. Durrell might well have been the constable in Van Horn, but that didn't mean he was honest. Ed Gray had been proof positive that a man with a star could be just as big an owlhoot as anybody. Durrell had missed out on that strongbox full of cash once in Van Horn when it was delayed, then again when he and Gray and the other two men had tried to stop the train. Longarm knew now what had happened to that fourth would-be robber. Then Durrell had used him to help find the women and the money, only to double-cross him now.

All that flashed through Longarm's brain in less than a heartbeat, and then the shooting started.

The rancher threw himself to the ground, out of the line of fire. Myra's gun blasted as Durrell swung his rifle away from Longarm and toward her. He staggered as Myra's bullet clipped his thigh, but he got off two shots, working the Winchester's lever with blinding speed. The slugs slammed into Myra's body and drove her back through the open doorway of the cabin.

Longarm went to one knee, bringing his gun around smoothly toward Durrell. The Colt bucked against his palm as he fired once, twice, a third time, tracking Durrell as he squeezed off the shots. The middle slug missed, but the first one and the third one crashed into Durrell's chest, staggering him. He stayed on his feet, though, working the lever of the rifle and firing from the hip. The bullet whined past Longarm's ear. Longarm fired again, a head shot this time. The bullet caught Durrell just above the right eye and snapped his head back before exploding out the back of his skull. Durrell folded up, dead before he hit the ground.

Longarm stood up and whirled toward the door of the cabin. Myra had pulled herself back up, and she stood there with her gun held loosely in her hand. The front of her blouse was covered with blood.

''Just like a man,'' she said. ''Stubborn as hell. . . .''

Then she pitched forward onto her face.

Longarm stepped over to her, kicked away the gun she had

dropped when she fell. He knelt beside her and put a couple of fingers on her neck, knowing there was no real point but doing it anyway. He straightened and holstered his gun.

"Don't move, mister."

Longarm looked over his shoulder at the rancher pointing the rifle at him and said, "Don't be a fool. It's over. Where's the other one?"

"Inside. She's hurt."

"I know. And the money?"

"I don't know anything about any money," said the rancher. "But there's some full saddlebags on the table. I haven't looked in them."

"Probably a good thing. I'm a deputy U.S. marshal. Name's Custis Long."

"Reuben," said the rancher. "Reuben Wood." He lowered the Henry rifle and wiped the back of his hand across his mouth. "I own this spread. That is, my wife and I do."

Longarm stepped to the doorway. He saw a woman he had never seen before, a frightened but still attractive brunette, standing beside a blanket-covered bunk with a pistol in her hand. Timothea lay on the bunk, seemingly unconscious.

"Mrs. Wood?" asked Longarm.

The brunette hesitated, then nodded.

"No need to worry now, ma'am. The shooting's all over. I'm a lawman."

"A . . . lawman?"

"Yes, ma'am. Deputy U.S. Marshal Custis Long." Longarm gestured at Timothea. "That's an escaped prisoner of mine."

"But . . . she's hurt. You can't take her."

There was genuine concern in the woman's voice, more so than would be normal if she and her husband had been taken prisoner by Myra and Timothea and forced to help them. Longarm suddenly remembered that sixth fugitive from the wrecked prison wagon, the one who had supposedly drowned in Diablo Creek and been buried by the others.

He took a deep breath as the rancher stepped into the cabin behind him. Wood was still carrying the Henry rifle. Longarm rubbed his jaw. There was more going on here than he knew about, he decided. But he was fairly certain of one thing: The only man Timothea had killed was Ed Gray, and that had been in self-defense. Besides, the crooked sheriff had needed killing.

Reuben Wood moved over beside the woman he claimed as his wife. Maybe she really was, for all Longarm knew. Wood put his left arm around the woman's shoulders. The Henry rifle was still in his right hand.

A smile plucked at Longarm's mouth. "I got to ask you folks for a big favor," he said.

"A favor," repeated Wood.

Longarm nodded. "That's right. That woman there in the bunk is in bad shape, and I don't want to try to take her back to Fort Stockton with me. You reckon you could take care of her until somebody comes back to get her?"

"I . . . I suppose we could do that," said Wood.

"Now, I have to warn you," went on Longarm, "I don't know how long that'll be. So you just nurse her back to health if you can and tell her to wait here until the law comes."

"What if she won't wait?" asked the woman.

Longarm shrugged. "Well, in that case, I don't reckon there'll be much you can do about it. She's a notorious desperado, you know, so I wouldn't want you to try to stop her. Might be dangerous."

Wood frowned. "I never heard of such an arrangement." His wife dug an elbow in his ribs as he spoke.

"Well, we just do the best we can," said Longarm. He looked back over his shoulder at Myra's body. "There's some burying to be done."

Wood handed the rifle to his wife. "I'll help you, Marshal. Reckon it's the least I can do."

Longarm turned toward the door, and as he passed the saddlebags, he said, "By the way, these *will* have to go with me when I leave."

"Take them," said the woman. "We don't want them, do we, Reuben?"

Wood shook his head and looked at her. "No, we don't. I reckon we've already got everything we need."

• • •

Longarm rode into Fort Stockton four days later. He'd taken his time coming back from the Davis Mountains.

Myra and Durrell were both buried on the hillside above the cabin where Reuben Wood and his wife lived. In the time Longarm had spent there, he had never asked the woman's name. He didn't want to know. He had the saddlebags full of money, and the way things had turned out, he supposed that was what really mattered to the law.

As Longarm neared the sheriff's office and jail, he saw the young man sitting in a chair on the porch stand up and stare at him. "Marshal Long?" Dewey asked, astonishment showing on his face.

Longarm swung down from the horse and lifted off the saddlebags. "Better lock these up in a safe place," he told Dewey. He handed them to the deputy, who had no choice but to extend his arms and take them.

"What . . . what is this?"

"The money from the train that was robbed between Sierra Blanca and Van Horn a week ago," Longarm told him. "Watch over it mighty close."

With the loaded-down Dewey trailing him, Longarm strode into the sheriff's office. He looked through an open door into the cell block and saw that all the cells were empty.

"What happened to your prisoners?"

"You mean the two women?" Dewey dumped the saddlebags on the desk. "Another prison wagon from El Paso came and picked them up to take them on to the penitentiary."

Longarm felt a twinge of regret. He would have enjoyed seeing Abigail and Deborah again, especially Abigail. It might've been nice to show her what he could do with his hands and feet untied for a change. But, well, she was an escaped murderer, after all, he told himself. Some things just weren't meant to be.

Longarm turned toward the door, then stopped. "Oh, yeah, I got one more thing for you," he said as he reached into his shirt pocket. He took something out and tossed it onto the desk. "I reckon you're better suited to wear it than the last fella."

It was a sheriff's badge.

Watch for

LONGARM AND THE DIARY OF MADAME VELVET

251st novel in the exciting LONGARM series
from Jove

Coming soon!